Eemaan **Made Easy - Part 2**

مَعْرِفَةُ ٱلْمَلَـٰئِكَةِ

Knowing the Angels

بسم الله الرحمن الرحيم

الإيمانُ مُيَسَّراً – الجُزْءُ الثاني

EEMAAN MADE EASY - PART 2

مَعْرِفَةُ ٱلْمَلَـٰٓئِكَةِ

KNOWING THE ANGELS

SECOND EDITION

مُحَمَّد ٱلجِبَالي

MUHAMMAD AL-JIBALY

مَنْشُوراتُ ٱلْكِتَابِ وَٱلسُّنَّة

AL-KITAAB & AS-SUNNAH PUBLISHING

Knowing the Angels
(Eemaan Made Easy - Part 2)
Second Edition (Reprinted April 2007)

19+109 p. 24 × 18 cm
ISBN 1-891229-82-6

Published by:
Al-Kitāb & as-Sunnah Publishing
USA PO Box 2542, Arlington, Texas, 76004
Lebanon-Beirut +961-3-046338
Saudi Arabia PO Box 5683, Madinah
+966-50-9600572 / 4-8466002, 4-8450539
www.kspublications.com
info@kspublications.com

Printed by:
Al-Maktab al-Islāmī
PO Box 11/3771, Beirut, Lebanon
+961-5-456280, 5-450657
www.almaktab-alislami.com
islamic_of@almaktab-alislami.com

TABLE OF CONTENTS

PREFACE

Opening Sermon

إِنَّ ٱلْحَمْدَ لِلهِ، نَحْمَدُهُ وَنَسْتَعِينُهُ وَنَسْتَغْفِرُهُ،
وَنَعُوذُ بِاللهِ مِنْ شُرُورِ أَنْفُسِنَا وَمِنْ سَيِّئَاتِ أَعْمَالِنَا .
مَنْ يَهْدِهِ ٱللهُ فَلاَ مُضِلَّ لَهُ، وَمَنْ يُضْلِلْ فَلاَ هَادِيَ لَهُ.

Al-hamdu lillaah. Indeed, all praise is due to Allaah. We praise Him and seek His help and forgiveness. We seek refuge with Allaah from our souls' evils and our wrong doings. He whom Allaah guides, no one can misguide; and he whom He misguides, no one can guide.

وَأَشْهَدُ أَنْ لاَ إِلَـهَ إِلاَّ ٱللهُ، وَحْدَهُ لاَ شَرِيكَ لَهُ.
وَأَشْهَدُ أَنَّ مُحَمَّداً عَبْدُهُ وَرَسُولُهُ.

I bear witness that there is no (true) god except Allaah — alone without any partners. And I bear witness that Muhammad (ﷺ) is His *'abd* (servant) and messenger. [1]

﴿يَا أَيُّهَا ٱلَّذِينَ آمَنُوا ٱتَّقُوا ٱللهَ حَقَّ تُقَاتِهِ،

1 The above two paragraphs, together with the following three portions of Qur'aan, are called *Khutbat ul-Haajah* (the Sermon of Need). Allaah's Messenger (ﷺ) often started his speeches with this sermon, and he was keen to teach it to his companions. The *hadeeth*s in this regard are recorded by Muslim, Aboo Daawood, an-Nasaa'ee, and others, and are narrated by Ibn Mas'ood, Ibn 'Abbaas, and others (رضي الله عنهم). A full discussion of the various reports of this sermon is provided by al-Albaanee in his booklet, "*Khutbat ul-Haajah*", published by al-Maktab ul-Islaamee, Beirut.

وَلاَ تَمُوتُنَّ إِلاَّ وَأَنْتُمْ مُسْلِمُونَ۝﴾ آل عمران ١٠٢

«O you who believe! Revere Allaah the right reverence, and do not die except as Muslims.» [1]

﴿يَا أَيُّهَا ٱلنَّاسُ ٱتَّقُوا رَبَّكُمُ ٱلَّذِي خَلَقَكُمْ مِنْ نَفْسٍ وَاحِدَةٍ، وَخَلَقَ مِنْهَا زَوْجَهَا، وَبَثَّ مِنْهُمَا رِجَالاً كَثِيرًا وَنِسَآءً، وَٱتَّقُواْ ٱللهَ ٱلَّذِي تَسَآءَلُونَ بِهِ وَٱلأَرْحَامَ، إِنَّ ٱللهَ كَانَ عَلَيْكُمْ رَقِيبًا۝﴾ النساء ١

«O people! Revere your Lord who has created you from a single soul, created from it its mate, and dispersed from both of them many men and women. Revere Allaah through whom you demand things from one another, and (cherish the ties of) the wombs. Indeed, Allaah is ever-watchful over you.» [2]

﴿يَاأَيُّهَا ٱلَّذِينَ ءَامَنُواْ ٱتَّقُواْ ٱللهَ وَقُولُواْ قَوْلاً سَدِيدًا۝ يُصْلِحْ لَكُمْ أَعْمَالَكُمْ، وَيَغْفِرْ لَكُمْ ذُنُوبَكُمْ، وَمَن يُطِعِ ٱللهَ وَرَسُولَهُ فَقَدْ فَازَ فَوْزًا عَظِيمًا۝﴾ الأحزاب ٧٠-٧١

«O you who believe! Revere Allaah and say just words. He will then rectify your deeds and forgive your sins. He who obeys Allaah and His Messenger has certainly achieved a great victory.» [3]

أَمَّا بَعْدُ، فَإِنَّ خَيْرَ ٱلْحَدِيثِ كِتَابُ ٱللهِ،
وَخَيْرَ الْهَدْيِ هَدْيُ مُحَمَّدٍ (ﷺ)، وَشَرَّ الأُمُورِ مُحْدَثَاتُهَا،
وَكُلَّ مُحْدَثَةٍ بِدْعَةٌ، وَكُلَّ بِدْعَةٍ ضَلالَةٌ، وَكُلَّ ضَلالَةٍ فِي ٱلنَّارِ.

---

1 *Aal 'Imraan* 3:102.
2 *An-Nisaa'* 4:1.
3 *Al-Ahzaab* 33:70-71.

Indeed, the best speech is Allaah's (ﷻ) speech; the best guidance is Muhammad's (ﷺ) guidance; and the worst matters (in creed or worship) are those innovated (by the people), for every innovated matter is a *bid'ah* (prohibited innovation), and every *bid'ah* is an act of misguidance that (whoever initiated it) will reside in the Fire. [1]

A Word to Parents and Educators

The Goals of True Education

True Education is that which improves a person's knowledge and understanding of his *Deen*. It makes him more aware of the purpose of his creation and his role in this life. It builds in his heart a strong belief that enables him to distinguish between the right and wrong, and a strong *eemaan* that compels him to abide by the right and refrain from the wrong.

True education is a social necessity. It is a prerequisite for attaining success and dignity similar to those that were enjoyed by the first Muslim generations.

Faults in Current Islaamic Curricula

It is indeed sad to see that education, with the above goals, has largely vanished from among the Muslims. Most of those who took its lead lack in clear Islaamic knowledge and vision. In their heart, there is a great void that they attempt to fill with numerous imported educational theories, causing a severe distortion to the Islaamic identity.

Verily, a quick review of the available Islaamic curricula, as well as the books available for children's reading, exposes an obvious problem. There is an serious confusion in determining the right approach and material to present to the children.

We find that the themes of many Islaamic children's books

1 Muslim and others have recorded from Jaabir Bin 'Abdillaah (ﷺ) that Allaah's Messenger (ﷺ) used to start his speeches with this paragraph.

revolve around magic and superstition, deviant beliefs and practices, historical falsehoods and slanders, offensive thought, or disguised invitations to religious or ideological beliefs that contradict Islaam!

Mending the Rift

All of this has prompted us to write for our beloved youth books meant to help in filling the current gaps and mending the current rifts.

In these books, as in the rest of our publications, we base the material that we present on the authentic sources: Allaah's Book, His Messenger's (ﷺ) Sunnah, and the clear understanding of the true scholars of Islaam.

In these books, we use easy language and present the concepts in a simplified manner. We do this without compromising the accuracy or breadth of coverage. This makes these books ideal as textbooks for elementary and intermediate school levels. In addition, their attractive appearance and numerous exercises make them useful sources of both knowledge and entertainment.

This publication is, therefore, a humble response to our realization of a great responsibility: the responsibility of bringing forth, before the English speaking youth, reading and study materials that refine the Islaamic concepts and present Islaam pure and simple, as close as possible to the way that it was understood and practiced by its early good pioneers - the *Salaf*.

Eemaan Made Easy

The "*Eemaan* Made Easy" series covers the six pillars of *Eemaan* mentioned in the *hadeeth* of Jibreel (عليه السلام) and elaborates on some subjects related to them. The material is well-founded on authentic proofs from the Qur'aan and Sunnah. The books are written in easy language, making them accessible to individuals with limited vocabulary.

This series covers the six pillars of *Eemaan* and related subjects as follows:

1. Knowing Allaah
2. Knowing the Angels
3. Knowing Allaah's Books & the Qur'aan
4. Knowing Allaah's Prophets & Messengers
5. Knowing the Last Day
6. Knowing Allaah's Decree — the *Qadar*

Each book is structured into chapters, sections, and subsection to organize learning and facilitate grasping the concepts. Furthermore, each chapter includes exercises to emphasize, review, and reinforce the concepts. All of this makes the *Eemaan Made Easy* series a valuable source of reliable study material for schools and individuals.

Technicalities

Translating and Transliterating Arabic

In our attempt to minimize the use of Arabic terms, we use transliterated Arabic terms in the following two situations only:

a) When no English expression is found that can reflect the same meaning as the original term.

b) When it is judged that an Arabic term is of such importance that it is essential to familiarize the reader with it.

At the end of this book, we have included a glossary defining common Arabic terms that fulfill the above criteria.

Except for proper nouns, transliterated Arabic terms are *italic*ized. In general, the rules of English pronunciation can be applied. The following table includes additional symbols employed in this book to help pronounce Arabic terms.

Symbol	Stands for	English Equivalent Sounds
aa, Aa	(ا) *Alif* (long vowel a)	Mostly: Man, sad. At times: Father, hard, god.
oo, Oo	(و) *Waaw* (long vowel u)	Root, soup, flute.
ee, Ee	(ي) *Yaa'* (long vowel i)	Seed, lean, piece, receive.
'	(ء) *Hamzah*	The first consonant vocal sound uttered when saying: at, it or oh.
Th, th	(ث) *Thaa'*	Three, moth.
H, h	(ح) *Haa'*	No equivalent. Produced in the lower throat, below "h". Resembles the sound produced after swallowing.
Kh, kh	(خ) *Khaa'*	No equivalent. Produced in the back of the mouth and top of the throat.
Th, th	(ذ) *Thaal*	There, mother.
S, s	(ص) *Saad*	A deeper "s" sound. Somewhat close to the "sc" in "muscle".
Dh, dh	(ض) *Dhaad*	Sounds deeper than a "d". Produced by touching the tongue to the mouth's roof.
T, t	(ط) *Tah*	Similar but deeper than a "t".
Z, z	(ظ) *Zah*	A deeper *thaal*, produced by touching the tip of the tongue to the back of the front teeth.
'	(ع) *'Ayn*	Produced in the bottom of the throat, underneath "h".

Symbol	Stands for	English Equivalent Sounds
Gh, gh	(غ) *Ghayn*	A gurgling sound produced in the back of the mouth, just above the *khaa'*. Similar to the "R" in some french accents.
Q, q	(ق) *Qaaf*	Somewhat similar to the "c" in "coffee".

TRANSLATING AND REFERENCING QUR'AAN AND *HADEETH*

The Qur'aan contains Allaah's exact words. These words cannot be exactly translated into other languages because of possible misinterpretations and limited human understanding. When an *aayah* is cited, the Arabic text is quoted followed, between double angle quotation marks, by the English meaning in «**boldface**». The meaning is extracted from books of *tafseer* and accessible translations.

The location of a Qur'aanic citation is specified in a footnote, providing the name of the *soorah*, its number, and the number(s) of the *aayah*(s) cited.

Similarly, the Arabic text of a *hadeeth* is quoted first. Its meaning is then presented in ‹**boldface**›, between single angle quotation marks. If the *hadeeth* relates a supplication, we usually present, as well, a full transliteration to help pronounce the supplication.

A footnote normally specifies the location of a cited *hadeeth* in the books of Sunnah, as well as its degree of authenticity and the names of scholars who made such a judgment.

NOTABLE UTTERANCES

Out of love, appreciation, gratitude or other noble feelings, a Muslim is encouraged to say certain phrases at the mention of Allaah, His messengers, the angels, the *sahaabah*, or other righteous Muslims. We present these phrases in condensed Arabic calligraphy as follows:

Phrase	Said after	Transliteration	Meaning
سبحانه وتعالى	Allaah's Name	*Subhaanahoo wa ta'aalaa.*	He is exalted above weakness and indignity.
عز وجل	Allaah's Name	*'Azza wa-jall.*	May He be exalted and glorified.
جل جلاله	Allaah's Name	*Jalla jalaaluh.*	May His glory be exalted.
صلى الله عليه وسلم	Muhammad or other prophets	*Salla 'Llaahu 'alayhi wa sallam.*	Allaah's peace and praise be on him.
عليه السلام	Prophets and angels	*'Alayh is-Salaam.*	Peace be on him.
رضي الله عنه	A male companion	*Radhiya 'Llaahu 'anhu.*	May Allaah be pleased with him.
رضي الله عنها	A female companion	*Radhiya 'Llaahu 'anhaa.*	May Allaah be pleased with her.
رضي الله عنهما	Two companion	*Radhiya 'Llaahu 'anhumaa.*	May Allaah be pleased with them.
رضي الله عنهم	Several companions	*Radhiya 'Llaahu 'anhum.*	May Allaah be pleased with them.
رحمه الله	A scholar or righteous Muslim.	*Rahimahu 'Llaah.*	May Allaah have mercy on him.

When coming across any of these symbols, the reader is advised to say the complete phrase in order to obtain the reward of saying the appropriate *thikr* or *du'aa'*.

Acknowledgements

All praise and thanks are due to our Lord (ﷻ) who facilitated completing this work. And may Allaah reward all the Muslims who helped and supported this effort in any way. In particular, may Allaah reward 'Abdullah al-Jibaly for designing the cover, and Aalaa' and Arwaa al-Jibaly for proofreading the manuscript.

We ask Allaah (ﷻ) to make this humble effort helpful and fruitful to the Muslims, forgive our shortcomings, purify our work from hypocrisy and conceit, and accept it from us.

Our Lord, forgive us and all of the believers, and bestow Your peace and praise upon our Prophet Muhammad (ﷺ).

Muhammad al-Jibaly
12 *Jumaadaa al-Aakhirah* 1424
11 August 2003

CHAPTER 1

THE SECOND PILLAR

The Six Pillars of Faith

In the first book of this series (Knowing Allaah), we discussed the Six Pillars of Faith. They were mentioned in the *hadeeth* of Jibreel (عليه السلام) — when he came to the Prophet (ﷺ) and asked him about Islaam, *Eemaan*, *Ihsaan*, and the Last Hour. The Six Pillars are:

1. Belief in Allaah
2. **Belief in the angels**
3. Belief in the books
4. Belief in the messengers
5. Belief in the Last Day
6. Belief in the *qadar*.

We must believe in all of these pillars. Allaah (سبحانه وتعالى) mentions the first four of them in the following *aayah*:

﴿ءَامَنَ ٱلرَّسُولُ بِمَآ أُنزِلَ إِلَيْهِ مِن رَّبِّهِۦ وَٱلْمُؤْمِنُونَ ۚ
كُلٌّ ءَامَنَ بِٱللَّهِ وَمَلَـٰٓئِكَتِهِۦ وَكُتُبِهِۦ وَرُسُلِهِۦ﴾ البقرة ٢٨٥

«The Messenger (Muhammad) believes in what was sent down to him from his Lord, and so do the believers. They all believe in Allaah, His angels, His books, and His messengers.» [1]

Allaah (ﷻ) also mentions five of them in the following:

﴿لَيْسَ ٱلْبِرَّ أَنْ تُوَلُّوا۟ وُجُوهَكُمْ قِبَلَ ٱلْمَشْرِقِ
وَٱلْمَغْرِبِ، وَلَٰكِنَّ ٱلْبِرَّ مَنْ ءَامَنَ بِٱللهِ وَٱلْيَوْمِ ٱلآخِرِ
وَٱلْمَلَٰٓئِكَةِ وَٱلْكِتَٰبِ وَٱلنَّبِيِّينَ، ...﴾ البقرة ١٧٧

«Righteousness does not (only) mean that you turn your faces toward east or west (in the prayer); righteousness is believing in Allaah, the Last Day, the angels, the books (of Allaah), and the prophets, ...» [2]

Anyone who does not believe in every single one of these pillars is not a true believer. Allaah (ﷻ) says:

﴿وَمَن يَكْفُرْ بِٱللهِ وَمَلَٰٓئِكَتِهِ وَكُتُبِهِ وَرُسُلِهِ وَٱلْيَوْمِ
ٱلآخِرِ فَقَدْ ضَلَّ ضَلَٰلًا بَعِيدًا ۝﴾ النساء ١٣٦

«Anyone who does not believe in Allaah, His angels, His books, His messengers, or the Last

1 *Soorat al-Baqarah* 2:285.
2 *Soorat al-Baqarah* 2:177.

Day, is surely greatly misguided.» [1]

Knowing the Angels

A true believer must believe in all of Allaah's angels. Believing in the angels is the second pillar of belief. This is our subject of study in this book.

The angels are beings that we cannot see. We only know about them as much as Allaah told us in His Book (the Qur'aan), or His Messenger Muhammad (ﷺ) told us in his Sunnah.

We should learn some of the angels' qualities, the jobs that Allaah (ﷻ) gave to them, and how they perform their jobs. By learning about the angels, we can answer many important questions. We can also learn what we should do to deserve the help and friendship of the angels.

When Were the Angels Created?

We do not know exactly when the angels were created. All we know is that Allaah (ﷻ) created them before humans. When Allaah (ﷻ) wanted to create humans and place them on earth, He told the angels about this, and they had a serious concer. Allaah (ﷻ) says:

---

1 *Soorat an-Nisaa'* 4:136.

﴿وَإِذْ قَالَ رَبُّكَ لِلْمَلَٰٓئِكَةِ إِنِّي جَاعِلٌ فِي ٱلْأَرْضِ خَلِيفَةً، قَالُوٓاْ أَتَجْعَلُ فِيهَا مَن يُفْسِدُ فِيهَا وَيَسْفِكُ ٱلدِّمَآءَ، وَنَحْنُ نُسَبِّحُ بِحَمْدِكَ وَنُقَدِّسُ لَكَ؟ قَالَ إِنِّي أَعْلَمُ مَا لَا تَعْلَمُونَ ۝﴾ البقرة ٣٠

«And (mention) when your Lord said to the angels, "I will surely place successors on earth." They said, "Will You place on it those who will cause corruption and shed blood, while we glorify You with praises and honor You? He said, "Indeed, I know that which you do not know." » [1]

This shows that the angels were created before Aadam (ﷺ). From what Allaah (ﷻ) taught them, they knew that humans are creatures that spread evil and killing on earth. They mentioned this to Allaah very politely. But Allaah knew better. He knew that some of the humans, such as the prophets and *sahaabah*, will be good individuals who will obey Allaah and strive for His cause.

Number of the Angels

There are many angels, and only Allaah (ﷻ) knows their number.

---

1 *Soorat al-Baqarah* 2:30.

Allaah (ﷻ) says about the angels who guard Hell:

﴿سَأُصْلِيهِ سَقَرَ ۝ وَمَآ أَدْرَاكَ مَا سَقَرُ ۝ لاَ تُبْقِي وَلاَ
تَذَرُ ۝ لَوَّاحَةٌ لِّلْبَشَرِ ۝ عَلَيْهَا تِسْعَةَ عَشَرَ ۝ وَمَا جَعَلْنَآ
أَصْحَـٰبَ ٱلنَّارِ إِلاَّ مَلَـٰئِكَةً وَمَا جَعَلْنَا عِدَّتَـهُمْ إِلاَّ فِتْنَةً
لِّلَّذِينَ كَفَـرُواْ﴾ المدّثر ٢٦-٣١

«I will throw him [1] into hell. And what will make you know exactly what is hell? It does not leave a thing (but burns it), and it turns the skins black. It has nineteen guards. We have not placed as the guards on the Fire except angels, and We have fixed their number only as a trial for the disbelievers.» [2]

These nineteen angels are enormous and have many helpers. When this *aayah* was revealed to Muhammad (ﷺ), Aboo Jahl made fun of it and said, "Muhammad has only nineteen helpers!" Allaah (ﷻ) then revealed:

﴿وَمَا يَعْلَمُ جُنُودَ رَبِّـكَ إِلاَّ هُوَ﴾ المدّثر ٣١

«No one knows the number of your Lord's soldiers except Him.» [3]

---

1 This refers to al-Waleed Bin al-Mugheerah, one of the most stubborn disbelievers from the Quraysh.

2 *Soorat al-Muddaththir* 74:26-31.

3 *Soorat al-Muddaththir* 74:31.

This means that the angel are among Allaah's soldiers, that they are very large in number, and that He alone knows their count. Also, the Prophet (ﷺ) said:

«يُؤْتى بجَهنّمَ يومَئذٍ لها سبعونَ ألفَ زِمامٍ،
مع كُلِّ زِمامٍ سبعونَ ألفَ ملَكٍ يَجُرّونَها.»

‹Hell will be pulled on the Day of Judgment with seventy thousand ropes, each rope held by seventy thousand angels.› [1]

This means that a total of about five billion powerful angels will be in charge of hell.

There are many other *hadeeth*s telling about the great number of angels. For example, the Prophet (ﷺ) said that the heavens are completely filled with angels praying to Allaah. He also said that every day seventy thousand additional angels make *hajj* to al-Bayt ul-Ma'moor [2] in the seventh heaven. And he mentioned that there are angels with every human being: two of them write all what he does, others tell him to do good, others protect him, and so on. [3]

Also, Aboo Hurayrah (رضي الله عنه) reported that the Prophet (ﷺ) said:

---

1 Recorded by Muslim and at-Tirmithee from Ibn Mas'ood (رضي الله عنه).

2 "Al-Bay ul-Ma'moor" means "The Full House of Worship". It is similar to the Ka'bah on earth. Angels go to it to worship Allaah.

3 These *hadeeth*s will be presented later in the book.

«ليلة القدر ليلةُ سابعةٍ أو تاسعةٍ وعشرينَ، إن الملائكةَ تلك الليلةَ في الأرضِ أكثرُ من عدد الحصى.»

‹*Laylat ul-Qadr* (the Night of Decree) is the night of the twenty-seventh or twenty-ninth (of *Ramadhaan*). Surely, during it, the angels on earth are more than the number of pebbles.› [1]

Therefore, the number of angels is far more than what we can imagine.

Names of the Angels

We only know the names of very few angels. In this book, we only accept the names that are mentioned in the Qur'aan or authentic Sunnah. Thus, even though many people think that "Radhwaan", "'Izraa'eel", and "Raqeeb and 'Ateed" are names of angels, we do not adopt this because of the lack of evidence.

Angels That We Know

In the Qur'aan, Allaah mentions the names of five angels: Jibreel, Meekaa'eel (or Meekaal), Maalik, Haaroot, and Maaroot.

1 Recorded by Ahmad, Ibn Khuzaymah, and others. Verified to be *hasan* (good) by al-Albaanee (*as-Saheehah* no. 2205).

Among the angels that are mentioned by name in the *hadeeths* of the Prophet (ﷺ) are Israafeel, Munkar, and Nakeer.

Some angels are mentioned in the Qur'aan or the Sunnah, but we are not told their names. For example, we are told about the Angel of Death, and the Angel of Mountains.

Is Satan an Angel?

Some people think that Iblees (or Satan) is an angel or that he used to be an angel because Allaah (ﷻ) says:

﴿وَإِذْ قُلْنَا لِلْمَلَـٰٓئِكَةِ ٱسْجُدُواْ لِأَدَمَ، فَسَجَدُواْ، إِلَّآ إِبْلِيسَ أَبَىٰ﴾ البقرة ٣٤

«And (mention) when We said to the angels, "Make *sujood* before Aadam." They all made *sujood* — except for Iblees, who refused.» [1]

But this *aayah* only tells us that Iblees used to be with the angels. Another *aayah* clearly tells us that Iblees was never an angel, but is actually from the *jinns*:

﴿وَإِذْ قُلْنَا لِلْمَلَـٰٓئِكَةِ ٱسْجُدُواْ لِأَدَمَ، فَسَجَدُواْ، إِلَّآ إِبْلِيسَ كَانَ مِنَ ٱلْجِنِّ فَفَسَقَ عَنْ أَمْرِ رَبِّهِ﴾ الكهف ٥٠

1 *Soorat al-Baqarah* 2:34.

«And (mention) when We said to the angels, "make *sujood* before Aadam." They all made *sujood,* except for Iblees who was from the *jinn*s and he disobeyed his Lord's order.» [1]

CARRYING AN ANGEL'S NAME

Is it permissible to carry an angel's name, such as Jibreel, Meekaa'eel, or Israafeel? Many of the *'ulamaa'* (scholars) dislike this because the *salaf* (the early Muslims) did not name their children such names, and we should always follow their example. For the same reason, it is disliked to name a girl Malak or Malaak, both of which meaning "angel".

However, it is permissible to use names that are not specific to angels, such as Maalik, which means "owner".

Where Are the Angels?

The angels usually stay in the heavens. They come down to earth when Allaah orders them. They also take things up to the heavens, like the good deeds of the people, and the souls of the dead. They sometimes come down in large numbers, as on *Laylat ul-Qadr*. Allaah (ﷻ) says about that:

﴿ تَنَزَّلُ ٱلْمَلَٰٓئِكَةُ وَٱلرُّوحُ فِيهَا بِإِذْنِ رَبِّهِم مِّن كُلِّ أَمْرٍ ۝ ﴾ القدر ٤

«The angels and the Spirit (Jibreel) descend

---

1 *Soorat al-Kahf* 18:50.

during it (*Laylat ul-Qadr*) with all sorts of orders — by their Lord's permission.» [1]

Do the Angels Die?

We do not know if the angels die during this life. Allaah did not tell us anything about this, and we may not say anything without knowledge.

But we know that at the end of time, the Last Day or the Dooms Hour, Allaah will make everyone die. He will remain by Himself. He will then give life back to everyone on the Day of Resurrection. Allaah (ﷻ) says:

﴿كُلُّ شَيْءٍ هَالِكٌ إِلاَّ وَجْهَهُ﴾ القصص ٨٨

«Everything will be destroyed except Allaah's Face.» [2]

Therefore, even the angels will die at that time.

Are the Angels Better than the Believers?

Who are better, the angels or the righteous believers? This is a controversial question that is of no real consequence. We present it here only because it is often raised by the scholars when discussing the angels.

---

1 *Soorat al-Qadr* 97:4.

2 *Soorat al-Qasas* 28:88.

The correct answer to this question is:

a. In this life, humans continually sin and disobey Allaah, but the angels never sin and they always obey and worship Allaah. Because of this, we say that the angels are better than most people.

b. In the hereafter, the righteous people will be better than the angels because they had passed the trial of this life. Allaah (ﷻ) has prepared for them great rewards in *Jannah*. When they enter it, large numbers of angels will welcome and serve them. Allaah (ﷻ) says:

﴿جَنَّٰتُ عَدْنٍ يَدْخُلُونَهَا وَمَن صَلَحَ مِنْ ءَابَآئِهِمْ وَأَزْوَٰجِهِمْ وَذُرِّيَّٰتِهِمْ وَٱلْمَلَٰٓئِكَةُ يَدْخُلُونَ عَلَيْهِم مِّن كُلِّ بَابٍ ۝ سَلَٰمٌ عَلَيْكُم بِمَا صَبَرْتُمْ فَنِعْمَ عُقْبَى ٱلدَّارِ ۝﴾ الرعد ٢٣-٢٤

«(The righteous believers) will enter everlasting gardens of 'Adn [1], together with those who were righteous of their fathers, wives, and children. The angels will come to them from every gate saying "*Salaamun 'Alaykum* — peace be upon you, because you were patient! Your final home is surely excellent!" » [2]

1 A name for the gardens of paradise.

2 *Soorat ar-Ra'd* 13:23-24.

Questions and Exercises

1. In the following table, check all true statements (19 points):

	Statement	✓
a	There are five pillars of faith.	
b	We do not have to believe in all of the pillars of faith.	
c	Belief in the angels is one of the pillars of faith.	
d	We can see the angels with binoculars.	
e	We know about the angels from the Qur'aan, the *hadeeth*s, and comics books.	
f	The angels were created before the people.	
g	The angels are better than people in this life.	
h	The angels serve the people of *Jannah*.	
i	We know the names of most angels.	
j	We can make up names for angels.	
k	The angels initially thought that it was not a good idea to create Aadam.	
l	The angels never die.	

	Statement	✓
m	A large number of angels comes down to earth on *Laylat ul-Qadr.*	
n	The angels count pebbles during *Laylat ul-Qadr.*	
o	Iblees was an angel.	
p	Iblees refused to make *sujood* to Aadam.	
q	Iblees was obedient to Allaah.	
r	It is disliked to be named after angels.	
s	The angels say *salaam* to the people of *Jannah.*	

2. Mention two benefits of learning about the angels (2 points):

1	
2	

3. Who besides Allaah knows the number of angels? (Put a ✓ next to the right answer; 2 points)

	The prophets		The believers
	The angels		No one

4. Where do the angels usually stay? (Put a ✓ next to the right answer; 2 points)

	On other planets		In caves
	In the heavens		In the ocean

5. Mention the names of six angels: (3 points)

1	4
2	5
3	6

6. On Judgment Day, hell will be pulled by: (Put a ✓ next to the right answer; 2 points)

	5 thousand angels		5 million angels
	5 billion angels		nineteen angels

7. Some of the people of *Jannah* will be joined by their relatives. Explain briefly how this happens. (3 points)

CHAPTER 2

QUALITIES OF THE ANGELS

Allaah created the angels different from us. We cannot see them, hear them, touch them, or subject them to any of our human senses.

How then can we learn about the angels? Like other matters of *ghayb* [1], we learn about them from what Allaah tells us in His Book, or what the Prophet Muhammad (ﷺ) tells us in his *hadeeth*s.

The Angels Vary in Status

There are many characteristics common to all angels. But this does not mean that all angels are identical. They vary in power, size, number of wings, and so on.

An important example of the diversity among the angels is that they are of different positions and status. Some of them are nearer to Allaah than others. Allaah (ﷻ) says:

﴿وَمَا مِنَّآ إِلاَّ لَهُ مَقَامٌ مَعْلُومٌ ۝ وَإِنَّا لَنَحْنُ ٱلصَّآفُّونَ ۝
وَإِنَّا لَنَحْنُ ٱلْمُسَـبِّحُونَ ۝﴾ الصَّافات ١٦٤-١٦٦

---

1 The things beyond our human senses.

«(The angels say:) "Each one of us surely has a known place. And we surely are the ones who line up (for prayer before Allaah). And we surely are the ones who glorify Allaah."» [1]

The best of angels are those who fought with the Muslims in the battle of Badr. Raafi' Bin Khadeej (ﷺ) reported that the Prophet (ﷺ) said:

«أتاني جبريلُ، فقال: "ما تَعُدُّونَ من شهِدَ بدراً فيكم؟" قلت: "خِيارَنا." قال: "كذلك هم عِندَنا خِيارُ الْملائكةِ."»

‹Jibreel came to me and said, "How do you recognize the Muslims who fought in the battle of Badr?" I replied, "They are the best among us." He said, "We too recognize the angels who fought in it as the best."› [2]

"Physical" Qualities of the Angels

Since the angels are part of *ghayb* that is beyond our physical world, they are not like anything we see around us. We have to keep this in mind when we discuss some of their qualities below. For example, we are told that they have wings, but this does not mean that their wings are similar to the wings of birds,

---

1 *Soorat as-Saaffaat* 37:164-166.

2 This *hadeeth* is recorded by al-Bukhaaree and Ibn Maajah.

bees, or airplanes.

THEY WERE CREATED FROM LIGHT

Allaah (ﷻ) created the angels from light. This is an example of how different they are from us and from other things that we know. 'Aa'ishah (رضي الله عنها) reported that the Prophet (ﷺ) said:

«خُلِقت الْملائكةُ من نور، وخُلق الجانُّ من مارجٍ من نار، وخُلق آدمُ مِمّا وُصِفَ لكم.»

‹The angels were created from light, the *jinns* were created from dark flames of fire, and Aadam was created from that which has been described to you (in the Qur'aan).› [1]

Therefore, unlike the angels, Allaah (ﷻ) created the *jinns* from the smoke of fire. Some of the *jinns* are good, others are bad. We mentioned earlier [2] that Shaytaan (Satan) is one of the *jinns*. In this life, we can neither see the angels nor the *jinns*.

THEY HAVE WINGS

The angels have wings. Some angels have two wings, some three, some four, and some many more. Allaah (ﷻ) says:

1 Recorded by Muslim and others.
2 In Chapter 1.

﴿ٱلْحَمْدُ لِلَّهِ فَاطِرِ ٱلسَّمَـٰوَٰتِ وَٱلْأَرْضِ، جَاعِلِ ٱلْمَلَـٰٓئِكَةِ
رُسُلًا أُوْلِيٓ أَجْنِحَةٍ مَّثْنَىٰ وَثُلَـٰثَ وَرُبَـٰعَ، يَزِيدُ فِي ٱلْخَلْقِ
مَا يَشَآءُ، إِنَّ ٱللَّهَ عَلَىٰ كُلِّ شَيْءٍ قَدِيرٌ﴾ فاطر ١

«All praise is to Allaah, Creator of the heavens and earth, who made the angels messengers with wings, two or three or four. He increases in the creation as He wills. Allaah surely has power over all things.» [1]

In particular, the Prophet (ﷺ) told us that Jibreel has six-hundred wings! [2]

Do the angels have feathery wings like birds? We cannot say this because Allaah did not give us such knowledge.

They Are Powerful

Some angels are stronger than anything we know in this world. For example, only eight angels bear the greatest of Allaah's creation: the Throne. Allaah (ﷻ) says:

﴿وَٱلْمَلَكُ عَلَىٰٓ أَرْجَآئِهَا، وَيَحْمِلُ عَرْشَ رَبِّكَ
فَوْقَهُمْ يَوْمَئِذٍ ثَمَـٰنِيَةٌ﴾ الحاقّة ١٧

«The angels will cover all of the Heaven's corners. And, on that Day, eight (angels) will

1 *Soorat Faatir* 35:1.

2 The *hadeeth* about this will be presented later.

carry the Throne of your Lord above them.» [1]

Allaah (ﷻ) tells us that the angels who are in charge of Hell are extremely strong:

﴿عَلَيْهَا مَلَٰٓئِكَةٌ غِلَاظٌ شِدَادٌ لَّا يَعْصُونَ ٱللَّهَ مَآ أَمَرَهُمْ وَيَفْعَلُونَ مَا يُؤْمَرُونَ ۝﴾ التحريم ٦

«In charge of it (Hell) are angels who are harsh and powerful. They do not disobey Allaah in what He commands them, but do as they are commanded.» [2]

THEY ARE LARGE

Some angels are larger than anything that we have seen. For example, the angels that carry Allaah's Throne are large beyond imagination. The Prophet (ﷺ) said:

«أذن لي أن أحدِّثَ عن أحدِ حَمَلَةِ العرش، رجلاهُ في الأرضِ السُفلى، وعلى قرنه العرشُ، وبين شحمةِ أُذُنيهِ وعاتِقِه خفقانُ الطيرِ سبعَمِائَةِ عامٍ، يقول: "سبحانك حيثُ كُنتَ."»

‹I have (Allaah's) permission to tell you about one of the angels who carry the Throne. His feet stand on the lowest ground and the

1 *Soorat al-Haaqqah* 69:17.
2 *Soorat at-Tahreem* 66:6.

Throne sits on his forehead. It takes a bird seven hundred years to travel from his earlobe to his shoulder. He (constantly) says, "Exalted are You (O Allaah) where you Are."› [1]

THEY ARE BEAUTIFUL

The guards of Hell and other angels of punishment are harsh and stern because this is part of their job.

But angels usually have a good appearance. This truth is commonly known and accepted by people. For example, the wealthy women at the time of the prophet Yoosuf (ﷺ) thought that he was so handsome that he must be an angel. Allaah (ﷻ) says about them:

﴿وَقُلْنَ حَـٰشَ لِلَّهِ مَا هَـٰذَا بَشَرًا ، إِنْ هَـٰذَا
إِلَّا مَلَكٌ كَرِيمٌ ۝﴾ يوسف ٣١

«They said, "Perfect is Allaah! This is not a human being. This is only a noble angel.» [2]

In particular, Jibreel is a good-looking angel. Allaah (ﷻ) says about him:

---

1 Recorded by at-Tabaraanee (in *al-Awsat*) from Anas (ﷺ). Verified to be authentic by al-Albaanee (*as-Saheehah* no. 150 and *Saheeh ul-Jaami'* no. 853). A similar *hadeeth* from Anas is recorded by Aboo Daawood, at-Tirmithee, and others, and verified to be authentic by al-Albaanee (*as-Saheehah* no. 151 and *Saheeh ul-Jaami'* no. 854).

2 *Soorat Yoosuf* 12:31.

﴿عَلَّمَهُ شَدِيدُ ٱلْقُوَىٰ ۞ ذُو مِرَّةٍ فَٱسْتَوَىٰ ۞
وَهُوَ بِٱلْأُفُقِ ٱلْأَعْلَىٰ ۞﴾ النجم ٥-٧

«It (the Qur'aan) is taught to him (to Muhammad) by one (angel) of great might. He has a beautiful form [1], as he appeared in the upper horizon.» [2]

THEIR COLOR

Many ignorant people think that all angels are white in color. However, we learn from the Sunnah that when the angels would appear to some people in this world, they would have colors that fit the occasion. When the Prophet (ﷺ) saw Jibreel for the first time, he was wearing green clothing. [3] Munkar and Nakeer are blue-black in color [4]. The angels of death come to the believers with white faces, and to the disbelievers with dark faces. [5]

THEY DO NOT BECOME HUNGRY, TIRED, OR BORED

The angels are always busy obeying Allaah's commands. Yet, they never need sleep or rest. They are never tired

---

1 This is the explanation of Ibn 'Abbaas (رضي الله عنه) for the Arabic word '*mirrah*'.
2 *Soorat an-Najm* 53:5-7.
3 Recorded by al-Bukhaaree from Ibn Mas'ood (رضي الله عنه).
4 The *hadeeth* about this is cited in Chapter 4.
5 A detailed discussion of this is presented in the Author's book, "Life in al-Barzakh".

from worshiping and obeying Allaah, as He (ﷻ) says:

﴿فَإِنِ ٱسْتَكْبَرُواْ ، فَٱلَّذِينَ عِندَ رَبِّكَ يُسَبِّحُونَ لَهُ بِٱلَّيْلِ وَٱلنَّهَارِ، وَهُمْ لَا يَسْـَٔمُونَ ۝﴾ فصلت ٣٨

«If they refuse (to obey), then those (angels) who are near your Lord glorify Him by night and by day, and they do not become weary.» [1]

THEY DO NOT EAT

Even though we cannot survive without food, Allaah (ﷻ) created the angels so that they never have to eat!

For example, Allaah (ﷻ) sent angels to tell Ibraaheem (عليه السلام) that his wife will bear a boy called Ishaaq. The angels came to him in the form of men. Thinking that they were ordinary guests, he hurried to honor and feed them, and he quickly cooked a fat calf and placed it before them. They refused to eat, which annoyed Ibraaheem (عليه السلام). But they told him not to worry, because they were angels sent by Allaah to him, and also to punish Loot's people:

﴿وَلَقَدْ جَآءَتْ رُسُلُنَآ إِبْرَاهِيمَ بِٱلْبُشْرَىٰ، قَالُواْ سَلَـٰمًا ، قَالَ

1 *Soorat Fussilat* 41:38.

سَلَٰمٌ، فَمَا لَبِثَ أَن جَآءَ بِعِجْلٍ حَنِيذٍ ۝ فَلَمَّا رَءَآ أَيْدِيَهُمْ
لَا تَصِلُ إِلَيْهِ نَكِرَهُمْ وَأَوْجَسَ مِنْهُمْ خِيفَةً، قَالُواْ لَا تَخَفْ
إِنَّآ أُرْسِلْنَآ إِلَىٰ قَوْمِ لُوطٍ ۝﴾ هود ٦٩-٧٠

«Surely, our messengers came to Ibraaheem with the good news (of a baby). They said, *"Salaam,"* and he said, *"Salaam."* He quickly brought a fat calf. When he saw that they did not extend their hands to it (to eat), he disliked that and expected some evil from them. They said, "Do not be afraid! We are angels sent to (punish) the people of Loot."» [1]

THEY TRAVEL FAST

The angels travel very fast. They travel between the heavens and earth in a short time, bringing down Allaah's orders, taking up records of our deeds, and so on.

The angels must then be faster than horses, rockets, sound, light, or anything else that we know. In our physical world, we say that nothing can travel faster than light. But the angels are not controlled by the laws of this world. Allaah (ﷻ) is the Creator of the world and its laws. He gives the angels speeds and powers that suit their missions.

---

1 *Soorat Hood* 11:69-70.

THEY TAKE DIFFERNET FORMS

The angels can change their form whenever Allaah wants them to do so. For example, Jibreel (عليه السلام) often came to the Prophet (ﷺ) and his companions in the form of a man, just as the angels came to Ibraaheem (عليه السلام) as men. And Allaah (سبحانه وتعالى) tells us that Jibreel (عليه السلام) came to Maryam in the form of a man:

﴿وَٱذْكُرْ فِي ٱلْكِتَٰبِ مَرْيَمَ، إِذِ ٱنتَبَذَتْ مِنْ أَهْلِهَا
مَكَانًا شَرْقِيًّا ۝ فَٱتَّخَذَتْ مِن دُونِهِمْ حِجَابًا، فَأَرْسَلْنَا
إِلَيْهَا رُوحَنَا فَتَمَثَّلَ لَهَا بَشَرًا سَوِيًّا ۝ قَالَتْ إِنِّي أَعُوذُ
بِٱلرَّحْمَٰنِ مِنكَ إِن كُنتَ تَقِيًّا ۝ قَالَ إِنَّمَآ أَنَا رَسُولُ رَبِّكِ
لِأَهَبَ لَكِ غُلَٰمًا زَكِيًّا ۝﴾ مريم ١٦-١٩

«And mention in the Book the story of Maryam, when she stayed away from her family in an eastern place (for worship) and set a curtain between her and them. We sent to her Our Spirit (Jibreel) who took before her the form of a complete human being. She said, "I surely ask the Most Merciful to protect me from you — and you should fear Allaah." He said, "I am only a Messenger from your Lord to grant you a good son."» [1]

1 *Soorat Maryam* 19:16-19.

THEY DO NOT HAVE GENDER

We talk about the angels using the male gender: "he", "his", "him", and so on. But this does not mean that the angels are male — nor are they female.

The disbelievers during the Prophet's (ﷺ) time said that the angels were the daughters of Allaah. It is not right to say that Allaah should have a child, whether male or female, because He is the Lord and Owner of everything. He does not have a child, nor does he need one. Allaah (ﷻ) says about the disbelievers:

﴿وَجَعَلُوا۟ ٱلْمَلَـٰٓئِكَةَ ٱلَّذِينَ هُمْ عِبَـٰدُ ٱلرَّحْمَـٰنِ إِنَـٰثًا ۚ أَشَهِدُوا۟ خَلْقَهُمْ ۚ سَتُكْتَبُ شَهَـٰدَتُهُمْ وَيُسْـَٔلُونَ ۝﴾ الزخرف ١٩

«They say that the angels, who are servants to the Most Merciful, are females. Did they witness their creation? Their saying will be recorded, and they will be questioned about it (on the Day of Judgment)!» [1]

Furthermore, we cannot say that the angels marry or have children, because nothing like this is mentioned in the Qur'aan or Sunnah.

THE ANIMALS CAN SEE THEM

The animals can see or hear things better than the people.

1 *Soorat az-Zukhruf* 43:19.

Sometimes, the animals can see the angels. Aboo Hurayrah (ﷺ) reported that the Prophet (ﷺ) said:

«إذا سمِعتُم صِياحَ الدِّيَكَةِ فَسَلوا اللهَ مِن فَضْلِه، فإنّها رأت مَلَكاً. وإذا سمعتم نهيقَ الْحَمير فتعوّذوا باللهِ مِنَ الشيطانِ، فإنّها رأت شيطاناً.»

‹When you hear the crowing of a rooster, ask Allaah for His favors, because the rooster saw an angel. And when you hear the braying of a donkey, ask Allaah to protect you from Satan, because the donkey saw a devil.› [1]

Character of the Angels

The angels are chosen by Allaah (ﷻ) to be among the best of His creation. He gave them the best character and behavior. Allaah (ﷻ) says:

﴿ٱللَّهُ يَصْطَفِي مِنَ ٱلْمَلَـٰٓئِكَةِ رُسُلًا وَمِنَ ٱلنَّاسِ، إِنَّ ٱللَّهَ سَمِيعٌۢ بَصِيرٌ۝﴾ الحج ٧٥

«Allaah chooses messengers from among the angels and from among the people. Indeed, Allaah is Hearing and Seeing.» [2]

1 Recorded by al-Bukhaaree and Muslim.
2 *Soorat al-Hajj* 22:75.

THEY ARE NOBLE AND GOOD

Allaah (ﷻ) made the angels a most noble and good creation. They are obedient and precise in fulfilling His commands. Thus, Allaah (ﷻ) entrusted to them the delivery of His messages to the prophets. He also entrusted them to care for the Qur'aan that is in the heavens [1]. Allaah (ﷻ) says:

﴿بِأَيْدِي سَفَرَةٍ ۞ كِرَامٍ بَرَرَةٍ ۞﴾ عبس ١٥-١٦

«It (the Qur'aan) is (carried) in the hands of messengers (angels) who are noble and good.» [2]

A person who is good in reading the Qur'aan will be with those righteous angels. Our Mother 'Aa'ishah (رضي الله عنها) reported that the Prophet (ﷺ) said:

«الماهرُ بالقرآنِ مع السفرةِ الكرامِ البررة. والذي يقرأ القرآنَ ويُتعتعُ فيهِ وهو عليه شاقٌّ له أجران.»

‹A person who is skillful (or good) in reading the Qur'aan is with the noble and good messengers (of the angels). And a person who stammers and has difficulty when reading the

1 The Qur'aan is preserved in al-Lawh ul-Mahfoodth, which is with the angels in the heavens. This is discussed in the third book of this series: "Knowing Allaah's Books".

2 *Soorat 'Abas* 80:15-16.

Qur'aan receives a double reward.› [1]

THEY KNOW AS MUCH AS ALLAAH TEACHES THEM

The angels receive their knowledge from Allaah (ﷻ). They cannot know more than what He teaches them, nor do they know any less than that. Allaah (ﷻ) says about them:

﴿قَالُواْ سُبْحَانَكَ لاَ عِلْمَ لَنَآ إِلاَّ مَا عَلَّمْتَنَا﴾ البقرة ٣٢

«They said, "Glory be to You! We have no knowledge except what You taught us.» [2]

THEY LIKE TO LISTEN TO *QUR'AAN*

The angels like to listen to good things and hate hearing bad things. They like to listen to Qur'aan and to the praise of Allaah. They hate listening to music, lies, and other things taught by *Shaytaan*.

When the Qur'aan is recited nicely and sincerely to please Allaah, the angels come close to listen to it. Aboo Hurayrah (ﷺ) reported that the Prophet (ﷺ) said:

«ما اجتمع قومٌ في بيت من بيوت الله، يتْلُونَ كتابَ اللهِ ويتدارسونه بينهم، إلا نزلت عليهم السكينةُ، وغَشِيَتْهم الرحمةُ، وحفّتهمُ الملائكةُ، وذكرهم اللهُ فيمن عِنده.»

1 This *hadeeth* was recorded by al-Bukhaaree and Muslim.
2 *Soorat al-Baqarah* 2:32.

‹When a group of people meet in one of Allaah's houses (or *masjids*) to recite Allaah's Book and study it, peace descends over them, mercy flows among them, the angels surround them, and Allaah praises them to those (angels) who are close to Him.› [1]

One of the *sahaabah* called Usayd Bin Hudhayr (ﷺ) was once reciting *Soorat al-Baqarah* at night while his horse was tied beside him. The horse suddenly became uneasy and started jumping. When he stopped reciting, the horse became quiet. When he resumed reciting, the horse became uneasy again. After repeating this a few times, he stopped reciting and looked up. He was amazed to see right above him something that looked like a big cloud of bright lamps rising up in the sky. The next morning, he told the Prophet (ﷺ) about this, and the Prophet (ﷺ) said:

«تِلكَ الْملائكةُ كانت تستمعُ لكَ، ولو قرأتَ لأصبحَتْ يراها الناسُ ما تستتِرُ منهم.»

‹Those were angels who came to listen to your reading. Had you kept on reciting until morning, they would have remained visible for the people to see them!› [2]

1 This *hadeeth* is recorded by Muslim and others.
2 Recorded by al-Bukhaaree.

'Alee (ﷺ) reported that the Prophet (ﷺ) said:

«إنَّ العبد إذا تسوّكَ ثمّ قام يصلّي أتاه الملَك فقام خلفه يستمع القرآن ويدنو، فلا يزال يستمع ويدنو حتى يضع فاه على فيه، فلا يقرأ آية إلا كانت في جوف الملَك، فطهِّروا أفواهَكم للقرآن.»

‹When a person uses *siwaak* [1] and then stands for the night prayer, angel comes and stands behind him. The angel listens to the Qur'aanic recitation and slowly moves closer. He continues to listen and move closer until he finally places his mouth against the mouth of the person. Every *aayah* that the person recites thereafter would go into the angel. Thus, clean your mouth when reciting Qur'aan.› [2]

This shows the importance of standing in the prayer with nice smelling breath. If we then properly recite Qur'aan, an honorable guest, an angel, would come to us and receive our recitation straight into his mouth so as to take it up to the heavens.

---

1 A stick used to brush the teeth and give the mouth a nice smell.

2 Recorded by al-Bayhaqee, al-Bazzaar, and others. Verified to be authentic by al-Albaanee (*as-Saheehah* no. 1213 and *Saheeh ut-Targheeb* no. 215).

THEY LIKE TO LISTEN TO <u>*TH*</u>*IKR*

The angels like to go to places where Allaah (ﷻ) is mentioned and praised [1]. The Prophet (ﷺ) said:

«إذا كان يومُ الجُمُعة، وقفَتِ الْملائِكةُ على باب الْمسجِدِ، يكتُبونَ الأوّلَ فالأوّلَ. فإذا خرجَ الإمامُ طَوَوْا صُحُفَهُم، يستمِعونَ الذِّكرَ.»

‹On *Jumu'ah* (Friday), the angels stand at the doors of the *masjid* and write the names of those who come first and those who come next. When the *imaam* arrives (to start the sermon), they fold up their sheets and listen to the <u>*th*</u>*ikr*.› [2]

Also, the Prophet (ﷺ) said:

«إنّ للهِ ملائكةً سياحينَ فِي الأرض فُضُلاً عن كُتّابِ الناس، يلتمِسونَ أهلَ الذِّكر، فإذا وجدوا قوماً يذكُرونَ اللهَ تنادَوا: "هلُمُّوا إلَى بُغيتِكُم." فيجيئُون فيحُفُّون

---

1 This is called <u>th</u>*ikr*.

2 Recorded by al-Bukhaaree, Muslim, and others from Aboo Hurayrah.

بهم إلَى السماءِ الدنيا. »

‹Other than the angels who record the deeds of people, there is a group of Allaah's angels who travel over the earth. They search for the people who mention Allaah (ﷻ). When they find a group of people doing this, they call each other, "Here is what you are looking for." Then they come and cover that group with their wings until they are stacked up to the sky.›

«فيقول اللهُ: "أيَّ شيءٍ تركتُم عبادي يصنعونَ؟" فيقولونَ: "تركناهم يحمَدونَك، ويُمَجِّدونك، ويذكُرونك." فيقول: "هل رأوني؟" فيقولونَ: "لا." فيقول: "فكيفَ لو رأَوْني؟" فيقولون: "لو رأوكَ لكانوا أشدَّ تحميداً وتمجيداً وذِكراً."»

‹When these angels return to the heavens, Allaah (ﷻ) asks them, "What did you leave My servants doing?" They say, "We left them praising You and glorifying You and mentioning You."

Allaah (ﷻ) then asks, "Have they seen Me?" The angels reply, "No." Allaah (ﷻ) says, "What would they have done if they could see Me?" The angels reply, "They would then be even more busy in their praise, glorification, and remembrance of

You."›

«فيقول: "فأيَّ شيءٍ يطلُبونَ؟" فيقولون: "يطلبون الجنّةَ."
فيقول: "وهل رأَوْها؟" فيقولون: "لا." فيقول: "فكيف
لو رأوها؟" فيقولون: "لو رأوها كانوا أشدَّ عليها حِرصاً،
وأشدَّ لها طلباً."»

‹Then Allaah asks, "What did they ask from Me?" The angels reply, "They asked for *Jannah*." Allaah says, "Have they seen it?" They answer, "No." Allaah says, "What would they have done if they had seen it?" The angels answer, "Had they seen it, they would desire it more eagerly, and would work harder to reach it."›

«فيقول: "ومن أيِّ شيءٍ يتعوَّذون؟" فيقولون: "من النارِ."
فيقول: "وهل رأَوْها؟" فيقولون: "لا." فيقول: "فكيف
لو رأوها؟" فيقولون: "لو رأوها كانوا أشدَّ منها هرباً وأشدَّ
منها خوفاً." فيقول: "إني أشهِدُكم أنّي قد غفرتُ لهم."
فيقولون: "فإنَّ فيهم فُلاناً الخطّاءَ، لم يُرِدهُم، وإنّما جاء
لِحاجةٍ." فيقول: "هم القومُ لا يشقى بهم جليسُهُم."»

‹Then Allaah asks, "From what thing did

they seek My protection?" The angels answer, "They sought protection from the Fire." Allaah says, "Have they seen it?" They answer, "No." Allaah says, "What would they have done if they had seen it?" The angels answer, "Had they seen it, they would have feared it and run from it even more."

Then Allaah (ﷻ) says, "Be My witnesses: I have forgiven them!"

The angels then says, "But among them was a sinner who is not one of them. He had simply come for something he needed." Allaah (ﷻ) says, "(I have forgiven him too.) Anyone who sits with those people will not be a loser."› [1]

This shows how blessed would a person be if he is able to sit and listen to the *thikr* so that the angles would encircle him and tell Allaah (ﷻ) about him.

THEY ARE SHY

The angels are shy from the righteous believers. They love them, respect them, and show humbleness in their presence. The Prophet (ﷺ) explained to his companions how the angels respected 'Uthmaan Bin 'Affaan (رضي الله عنه). He said:

1 Recorded by al-Bukhaaree and Muslim from Aboo Hurayrah (رضي الله عنه).

«ألا أستحيي ممن استحيى منه الملائكة؟»

‹Should I not be shy of this man, when even the angels are shy of him?› [1]

THEY HATE BAD SMELLS

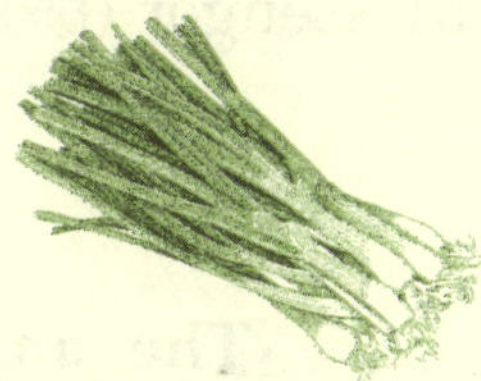

The angels are displeased and offended by ugly things that normal humans dislike, such as bad smells, spit, filth, and so on. Jaabir, Anas, and other *sahaabah* (ﷺ) reported that Allaah's Messenger (ﷺ) said:

«من أكلَ الثومَ والبصلَ والكرّاثَ فلا يقربَنَّ مسجِدنا ،
فإنَّ المَلائِكةَ تتأذّى مِمّا يتأذّى منهُ بنو آدمَ .»

‹When a person eats garlic, onions, or other evil-smelling foods, he should not come near our *masjid*. Surely, the angels dislike the same things that human beings dislike.› [2]

THEY DO NOT LIKE DOGS, PICTURES, OR BELLS

The angels do not enter houses that have dogs, bells, or pictures of human beings or animals. Aboo Talhah and 'Alee (ﷺ) reported that the Prophet (ﷺ) said:

---

1 Recorded by Muslim and others from 'Aa'ishah (ﷺ).
2 This *hadeeth* is recorded by al-Bukhaaree, Muslim, and others.

«إن الملائكة لا تدخل بيتاً فيه كلبٌ أو صورة.»

‹Surely, the angels do not enter into a house that has a dog or a picture.› [1]

Once 'Aa'ishah (ﷺ) saw a young girl wearing an anklet with ringing bells. 'Aa'ishah said that she heard Allaah's Messenger (ﷺ) say:

«لا تدخل الملائكة بيتاً فيه جرس.»

‹The angels do not enter into a house in which there is a bell.› [2]

The angels would not even accompany travelers who have these things. Aboo Hurayrah (ﷺ) reported that Allaah's Messenger (ﷺ) said:

«لا تصحَبُ الملائكةُ رُفقةً فيها كلب أو جرس.»

‹The angels do not join a company of people who have with them a dog or a bell.› [3]

Thus, if we want the best creation to be around us, we should avoid all that offends them.

---

1 Recorded by al-Bukhaaree, Muslim, and others.

2 This *hadeeth* was recorded by Aboo Daawood. It was verified to be *hasan* (good) by al-Albaanee (*Saheeh ut-Targheeb wat-Tarheeb* no. 3120).

3 Recorded by Muslim, Aboo Daawood, and others. There are similar reports from other *sahaabah* including 'Aa'ishah, Umm Habeebah, Anan, and Ibn 'Umar (ﷺ).

Questions and Exercises

1. In the following table, check all true statements (34 points):

	Statement	✓
a	The *jinn*s are different from the angels.	
b	All angels have two wings.	
c	Some angels are better than others.	
d	The best *sahaabah* are those who fought in Badr.	
e	The angels are very strong.	
f	The wings of angels are full of feathers.	
g	Some angels are huge.	
h	Most of the angels are male.	
i	Allaah has no children.	
j	The angels are white in color.	
k	The angels are beautiful.	
l	The angels sit down when they eat or drink.	
m	The angels sleep on their right side.	
n	All angels are identical.	

	Statement	✓
o	When the angels are bored, they play chess.	
p	Jibreel came to Maryam in the form of a man.	
q	The angels gave Ibraaheem good news.	
r	The angels took good news to the people of Loot.	
s	Ibraaheem's guests refused to eat the meat because it was not well cooked.	
t	The angels can travel very fast.	
u	The animals can sometimes see the angels.	
v	The animals cannot see the *jinns*.	
w	The angels can appear in the form of people.	
x	Jibreel is the angel with the most children.	
y	The angels like to listen to Qur'aan and *thikr*.	
z	The angels know only what Allaah teaches them.	
A	The angels are noble and good.	
B	The angels like to listen to soft music and singing.	
C	The angels are shy of good people.	
D	On *Jumu'ah*, the angels write the names of the people who come early to the *masjid*.	
E	The angels like the ringing of bells.	

	Statement	✓
F	The angels do not enter into a house that has a dog or a picture.	
G	The angels hate the smell of onions, garlic, cigarettes, and other bad smells.	
H	Nice breath is important before reciting Qur'aan.	

2. Match the types of creation (left) with the substance from which they were created (right) (3 points):

❶	The angels
❷	The *jinns*
❸	Human beings

①	Clay
②	Light
③	Smoke of fire

3. Answer the following questions regarding Usayd Bin Hudayr (ﷺ) (6 points):

a. Why did he stop reciting Qur'aan?	
b. What did he see in the sky?	
c. What would have happened if he kept reading?	

4. Answer the following questions regarding the angels who travel over the earth (10 points):

a. When do they call each other?	
b. What do they do to those mentioning Allaah?	
c. What would the believers have done if they saw Allaah?	
d. What would the believers have done if they saw *Jannah*?	
e. What would the believers have done if they saw the Fire?	

5. The number of angels who will carry the Throne on Judgment Day is: (Put a ✓ next to the right answer; 2 points)

	8 million		8 thousand		8

CHAPTER 3

WHAT THE ANGELS DO

In the last chapter, we focused on the angels' qualities. In this chapter, we focus on actions that are common to all angels. In the next chapter, we discuss actions specific to certain angels.

How the Angels Behave with Allaah

THEY ARE CLOSE TO ALLAAH

The angels are among the best of Allaah's creation. Because of this, He gave them important duties and allowed many of them to be close to Him. Allaah (ﷻ) says:

﴿لَن يَسْتَنكِفَ ٱلْمَسِيحُ أَن يَكُونَ عَبْدًا لِّلَّهِ،
وَلَا ٱلْمَلَٰٓئِكَةُ ٱلْمُقَرَّبُونَ﴾ النساء ١٧٢

«Al-Maseeh [1] will never refuse to be a servant to Allaah, nor will the angels who are near (to Allaah).» [2]

---

1 Al-Maseeh (or the Messiah) is a name for 'Eesaa (or Jesus).

2 *Soorat an-Nisaa'* 4:172.

THEY CONSTANTLY WORSHIP ALLAAH

The angels constantly worship Allaah, praying to Him, glorifying Him, praising Him, making *hajj* (pilgrimage) to al-Bayt ul-Ma'moor, and so on. Allaah (ﷻ) says:

﴿وَمَنْ عِندَهُۥ لَا يَسْتَكْبِرُونَ عَنْ عِبَادَتِهِۦ وَلَا يَسْتَحْسِرُونَ ۝ يُسَبِّحُونَ ٱلَّيْلَ وَٱلنَّهَارَ لَا يَفْتُرُونَ ۝﴾ الأنبياء ١٩–٢٠

«Those (angels) near Him are never too proud to worship Him, nor do they become tired (of the worship). They exalt Him night and day without reducing their worship.» [1]

The Prophet (ﷺ) explained what the angels say in their exaltation:

«أفضلُ الذِّكرِ ما اصطفى اللهُ لِملائكَتِه: "سُبحَانَ اللهِ وبِحَمدِه."»

‹The best way of *thikr* (remembering Allaah) is that which He chose for His angels, "*Subhaan Allaahi wa-bihamdih* — Glory be to Allaah, and I praise Him.› [2]

THEY PRAY IN STRAIGHT LINES

The angels pray to Allaah (ﷻ) in straight lines, just as we

1 *Soorat al-Anbiyaa'* 21:19-20.
2 Recorded by Muslim from Aboo Tharr (رضي الله عنه).

should. Allaah (ﷻ) says:

﴿وَٱلصَّٰٓفَّٰتِ صَفًّا ۝ فَٱلزَّٰجِرَٰتِ زَجْرًا ۝
فَٱلتَّٰلِيَٰتِ ذِكْرًا ۝﴾ الصّافات ١-٣

«By the angels who are lined up in rows (before Allaah), and who drive (the clouds) along, and who recite the Qur'aan ...» [1]

Once the Prophet (ﷺ) told his companions:

«ألا تَصُفُّونَ كما تَصُفُّ الْمَلائِكَةُ عِندَ رَبِّها؟
يُتِمُّونَ الصَّفَّ الأوَّلَ فالأول، ويتراصّونَ في الصَّفِّ.»

‹Don't you like to line up like the angels line up before their Lord? They complete the first row, then the next.› [2]

THEY MAKE *SUJOOD*

The angels pray to Allaah standing, bowing, and making *sujood*. The Prophet (ﷺ) said:

«أطّتِ السّماءُ، ويَحِقُّ لها أن تَئِطَّ، ما فيها موضعُ شبرٍ
إلا وعليهِ ملَكٌ ساجدٌ أو قائمٌ يُسَبِّحُ اللهَ بحمدِه.»

---

1 *Soorat as-Saaffaat* 37:1-3.
2 Recorded by Muslim and others from Jaabir Bin Samurah (رضي الله عنه)

‹The heavens have squeaked (from weight), and they have a right to squeak. There is not even a span [1] but that it has an angel in *sujood* or standing (in prayer), exalting and praising Allaah.› [2]

THEY GO FOR *HAJJ*

The angels visit al-Bayt ul-Ma'moor to worship Allaah (ﷻ). Every day, seventy thousand of them enter it and never come back again until the Day of Judgment. The Prophet Muhammad (ﷺ) said:

«البيتُ الْمعمورُ في السماءِ السابعةِ، يدخُلُهُ كُلَّ يومٍ سبعونَ ألفَ ملَكٍ، ثمّ لا يعودونَ إليهِ حتّى تقومَ الساعةُ.»

‹Al-Bayt ul-Ma'moor is in the seventh heaven. Seventy thousand angels enter it every day and never return to it until the Last Hour.› [3]

1 Approximately nine inches (22 cm).

2 Recorded by at-Tahaawee, at-Tabaraanee, and others from Anas and Hakeem Bin Hizaam (ﷺ). Verified to be authentic by al-Albaanee (*as-Saheehah* no. 852 and *Saheeh ul-Jaami'* no. 1020).

3 Recorded by Ahmad and an-Nasaa'ee from Anas (ﷺ) and verified authentic by al-Albaanee (*Saheeh ul-Jaami'* no. 2891). The same meaning is also recorded by al-Bukhaaree and Muslim from Anas.

THEY FEAR ALLAAH

Allaah deserved to be feared; and the angels know Him so well that they truly fear Him. Allaah (ﷻ) says:

﴿وَلِلَّهِ يَسْجُدُ مَا فِي ٱلسَّمَٰوَٰتِ وَمَا فِي ٱلْأَرْضِ مِن دَآبَّةٍ وَٱلْمَلَٰٓئِكَةُ وَهُمْ لَا يَسْتَكْبِرُونَ ۝ يَخَافُونَ رَبَّهُم مِّن فَوْقِهِمْ وَيَفْعَلُونَ مَا يُؤْمَرُونَ ۝﴾ النحل ٤٩-٥٠

«To Allaah bow (in *sujood*) all the living creatures in the heavens and on earth. The angels do too, without any arrogance. They fear their Lord above them, and they do as they are commanded (by Him).» [1]

The Prophet (ﷺ) describes Jibreel's fear of Allaah:

«مررتُ بجبريل ليلةَ أُسرِيَ بي بالْملأِ الأعلى، وهو كالحِلسِ البالي من خشيةِ الله عز وجل.»

‹On the night of *Israa'*, I passed by the highest angels. Jibreel looked like a worn-out rug from fearing Allaah (ﷻ).› [2]

1 *Soorat an-Nahl* 16:49-50.

2 Recorded by at-Tabaraanee (in *al-Awsat*) and al-Bazzaar from Jaabir (رضي الله عنه). Verified to be authentic by al-Albaanee (*as-Saheehah* no. 2289).

THEY OBEY ALLAAH

We have seen that the angels are most obedient to Allaah (ﷻ) and never disobey Him. Allaah also says:

﴿بَلْ عِبَادٌ مُكْرَمُونَ ۞ لاَ يَسْبِقُونَهُ بِٱلْقَوْلِ، وَهُم بِأَمْرِهِ يَعْمَلُونَ ۞﴾ الأنبياء ٢٦-٢٧

«They are only honored servants (to Allaah). They cannot speak before Him, and they act by His command.» [1]

THEY LOVE WHAT ALLAAH LOVES

The angels love what Allaah loves. So they love the people whom Allaah (ﷻ) loves. The Prophet (ﷺ) said:

«إن اللهَ تعالَى إذا أحبَّ عبداً دعا جبريلَ فقال: "إني أحبُّ فُلانًا فأحِبَّه." فيحبُّه جبريل. ثمّ يُنادي فِي السماءِ فيقول: "إنَّ اللهَ تعالَى يحبُّ فلانًا فأحِبّوه." فيحبّه أهلُ السماءِ، ثمّ يوضعُ له القَبولُ فِي الأرض. وإذا أبغضَ اللهُ عبداً دعا جبريلَ فيقولُ: "إنّي أُبغِضُ فُلانا فأبغِضْه." فيُبغِضُه جبريلُ، ثمّ ينادِي فِي أهلِ السماءِ: "إن اللهَ يُبغِضُ فلاناً

1 *Soorat al-Anbiyaa'* 21:26-27.

فأبغِضوهُ." فيُبغِضونه. ثم يوضعُ له البغضاءُ فِي الأرض.»

‹Indeed, when Allaah loves a (good) person, He calls to Jibreel (ﷺ), "I love so-and so, so love him." Jibreel loves him and calls out in the heavens, "Allaah loves so-and-so, so love him." The angels of the heavens love him, and acceptance is laid down for him on earth.

And when Allaah hates a (bad) person, He calls to Jibreel, "I hate so-and-so, so hate him." Jibreel then hates him and calls out in the heavens, "Allaah hates so-and-so, so hate him." The angels of the heavens hate him, and hatred is laid down for him on earth.› [1]

We saw earlier that the angels also love gathering that Allaah (ﷻ) loves. They like to accompany those who pray, recite Qur'aan, mention Allaah, or do other good deeds.

From this, we see the great falsehood of the myth about an angel of love called Cupid. He is pictured as a young naked boy carrying a bow and arrows. When he shoots an arrow at two individuals, they immediately fall in love. True angels only love and bring love with Allaah's permission.

They Only Descend with Allaah's Permission

The angels cannot descend from the heavens whenever they wish, but only when Allaah (ﷻ) tells them. Ibn

1 Recorded by Muslim and others, from Aboo Hurayrah (رضي الله عنه).

'Abbaas (ﷺ) reported that the Messenger of Allaah (ﷺ) said to Jibreel, «ألا تزورنا أكثرَ مِمّا تزورُنا؟» ‹**Why don't you visit us more often?**› Allaah (ﷻ) then revealed:

﴿وَمَا نَتَنَزَّلُ إِلاَّ بِأَمْرِ رَبِّكَ، لَهُ مَا بَيْنَ أَيْدِينَا وَمَا خَلْفَنَا﴾ مريم ٦٤

«We (angels) only descend by your Lord's command. To Him belongs that which is before us and that which is behind us.» [1] [2]

The Angels with the People

They Bring Down Allaah's Messages

Allaah (ﷻ) selected the angels for a very great and noble job, which is taking His commands and teachings to the people. Allaah (ﷻ) says:

﴿ٱلْحَمْدُ للهِ فَاطِرِ ٱلسَّمَـٰوَٰتِ وَٱلأَرْضِ، جَاعِلِ ٱلْمَلَـٰئِكَةِ رُسُلاً ... ﴾ فاطر ١

«All praise is to Allaah, the Creator of the heavens and earth, the One who has made the angels messengers ...» [3]

The angels deserved this great responsibility because of their wonderful qualities that we discussed earlier.

1 *Soorat Maryam* 19:64.
2 This *hadeeth* is recorded by al-Bukhaaree.
3 *Soorat Faatir* 35:1.

They Blow Life into People and Record their Future

While we are in our mother's womb, Allaah (ﷻ) sends an angel to blow life into us and write important things from our future. The Prophet (ﷺ) said:

«إن خلقَ أحدِكم يُجمَعُ في بطنِ أمِّه أربعين يوماً نطفةً، ثم يكونُ علقة مثلَ ذلك، ثم يكون مضغةً مثل ذلك، ثم يبعث إليه ملَكاً، فينفخ فيه الروح، ويؤمرُ بأربعِ كلماتٍ: بكتبِ رزقِه وأجلِه وعملِه وشقيٌّ أم سعيد.»

‹The creation of each one of you is brought together in his mother's womb for forty days as a seed, then as a clot for as long, then as a lump (of flesh) for as long. Allaah then sends an angel who is commanded to blow the soul into him and write down four things: his sustenance, life-span, deeds, and whether he will be miserable or happy.› [1]

They Write What the People Do

There are angels who stay with us at all times. They record all what we do, whether good or bad. Allaah (ﷻ) says:

﴿أَمْ يَحْسَبُونَ أَنَّا لاَ نَسْمَعُ سِرَّهُمْ وَنَجْوَاهُمْ؟ بَلَىٰ

1 Recorded by al-Bukhaaree and Muslim from Ibn Mas'ood (رضي الله عنه).

وَرُسُلُنَا لَدَيْهِمْ يَكْتُبُونَ ۝﴾ الزخرف ٨٠

«Did they think that We do not hear their secrets and private talks? Yes indeed! And Our messengers are by them to record.» [1]

These angels are most noble, and do not forget to write a thing. Every person in this life has two angels: one on his right recording his good deeds, and one on his left recording his bad deeds. Allaah (ﷻ) says:

﴿وَإِنَّ عَلَيْكُمْ لَحَـٰفِظِينَ ۝ كِرَامًا كَـٰتِبِينَ ۝
يَعْلَمُونَ مَا تَفْعَلُونَ ۝﴾ الإنفطار ١٢-١١

«Surely, there are (angels) appointed over you to watch you. They are honorable recorders. They know all that you do.» [2]

Also, Allaah (ﷻ) says:

﴿إِذْ يَتَلَقَّى ٱلْمُتَلَقِّيَانِ عَنِ ٱلْيَمِينِ وَعَنِ ٱلشِّمَالِ قَعِيدٌ ۝
مَا يَلْفِظُ مِن قَوْلٍ إِلَّا لَدَيْهِ رَقِيبٌ عَتِيدٌ ۝﴾ ق ١٨-١٧

«(We know) when the two receiving (angels) write, seated on the right and on the left. He (the person) does not utter one word but that

---

1 *Soorat az-Zukhruf* 43:80.
2 *Soorat al-Infitaar* 82:10-12.

with him is an observer ready (to write it).» [1]

The angel on the left gives a person a chance to repent from his sin before he records it for him. Aboo Umaamah (ﷺ) reported that the Prophet (ﷺ) said:

«إنّ صاحِبَ الشِّمال لِيَرفَعُ القَلَمَ سِتَّ ساعاتٍ عن العبدِ المُسلِمِ المُخْطِئِ، فإن ندِمَ واستغْفَرَ اللهَ مِنها ألقاها، وإلاّ كُتِبَتْ واحِدَةً.»

‹Indeed, the angel of the left lifts the pen for six hours from a sinful Muslim. If he then regrets and seek Allaah's forgiveness for his sin, the angel drops it. Otherwise, he records it as one wrong.› [2]

Similar to a *hadeeth* that we cited earlier [3], Aboo Umaamah (ﷺ) reported that the Prophet (ﷺ) said:

«إنّ المَلائكةَ ليقومونَ يوم الجُمُعةِ على أبواب المسجِدِ، معهُمُ الصّحُفُ، يكتُبونَ الناسَ الأوّلَ والثاني والثالِثَ، حتى إذا خرج الإمامُ طُوِيَتِ الصّحُف.»

‹On *Jumu'ah* (Friday), the angels stand at the

1 *Soorat Qaaf* 50:17-18.

2 Recorded by at-Tabaraanee, al-Bayhaqee, and Aboo Nu'aym. Verified to be *hasan* by al-Albaanee (*as-Saheehah* no. 1209 and *Saheeh ul-Jaami'* no. 2097).

3 In Chapter 2.

> **doors of the *masjid* holding records. They write the names of those who come first and second and third. When the *imaam* arrives (to give the *khutbah*), they fold up the records.›** [1]

When we realize that there are two angels seeing and writing all that we do, this will encourage us to do more good deeds and avoid sinning.

The Angels with the Believers

The angels are friends of the believers. They do everything they can in order to help and protect them.

THEY MAKE *DU'AA'* FOR THE BELIEVERS

The angels make *du'aa'* for the believers. They also make *du'aa'* for the believers who perform specific acts of worship. We will see examples in the following.

General *Du'aa'* for the Believers. The angels ask Allaah to forgive the believers, protect them from the punishment, and admit them into *Jannah*. Allaah (ﷻ) says:

﴿ٱلَّذِينَ يَحْمِلُونَ ٱلْعَرْشَ وَمَنْ حَوْلَهُۥ يُسَبِّحُونَ بِحَمْدِ رَبِّهِمْ،

---

1 Recorded by Ahmad and at-Tabaraanee. Verified to be *hasan* (good) by al-Albaanee (*Saheeh ut-Targheeb* no. 710 and *Saheeh ul-Jaami'* no. 1958).

وَيُؤْمِنُونَ بِهِۦ وَيَسْتَغْفِرُونَ لِلَّذِينَ ءَامَنُوا۟ : رَبَّنَا وَسِعْتَ كُلَّ
شَيْءٍ رَّحْمَةً وَعِلْمًا فَٱغْفِرْ لِلَّذِينَ تَابُوا۟ وَٱتَّبَعُوا۟ سَبِيلَكَ وَقِهِمْ
عَذَابَ ٱلْجَحِيمِ ۝ رَبَّنَا وَأَدْخِلْهُمْ جَنَّـٰتِ عَدْنٍ ٱلَّتِي وَعَدتَّهُمْ
وَمَن صَلَحَ مِنْ ءَابَآئِهِمْ وَأَزْوَٰجِهِمْ وَذُرِّيَّـٰتِهِمْ، إِنَّكَ أَنتَ ٱلْعَزِيزُ
ٱلْحَكِيمُ ۝ وَقِهِمُ ٱلسَّيِّـَٔاتِ، وَمَن تَقِ ٱلسَّيِّـَٔاتِ يَوْمَئِذٍ فَقَدْ
رَحِمْتَهُۥ، وَذَٰلِكَ هُوَ ٱلْفَوْزُ ٱلْعَظِيمُ ۝﴾ غافر ٧–٩

«The angels who carry the Throne and those around it exalt and praise their Lord and believe in Him and ask forgiveness for the believers, saying, "Our Lord, You surround all things with mercy and knowledge; forgive those who repent and follow Your way, and protect them from the punishment of the great Fire. Our Lord, admit them to the Gardens of 'Adn that You have promised them and whoever was righteous among their parents, spouses, and children. You are surely the Mighty and Wise. And protect them from all harm. Anyone whom You protect from harm on that Day will surely receive Your mercy, and that is the great success."» [1]

Waiting in the *Masjid* for the Prayer. The angels make *du'aa'* for a person who goes to the *masjid* early and waits for the

1 *Soorat Ghaafir* 40:7-9.

prayer to start. The Prophet (ﷺ) said:

«لا يزالُ العبدُ في صلاةٍ ما كان في مُصلاهُ ينتظرُ الصلاةَ، وتقول الْملائكةُ: "اللّهمّ اغفِر لهُ، اللّهمَّ ارحِمْهُ." حتى ينصرِفَ أو يُحْدِثَ.»

‹A person remains (as though) in prayer while he sits in the *masjid* waiting for the prayer. The angels continue to say, "O Allaah, forgive him; O Allaah, show mercy to him," unless he leaves or breaks his *wudoo'*.› [1]

Sitting for *Thikr* after the Prayer. After finishing the prayer, a Muslim should try to stay in his place for some time to make *thikr* or read Qur'aan. When he does this, the angels keep making *du'aa'* for him. The Prophet (ﷺ) said:

«الْملائكةُ تصلّي على أحدِكم ما دامَ في مُصلاّه الذي صلّى فيه، ما لم يُحدِث أو يَقُم: "اللهمّ اغفِر له، اللهمّ ارحَمْهُ."»

‹The angels pray for any of you who remains in his place after the prayer, as long as he keeps his *wudoo'* and does not leave. They say, "O Allaah, forgive him; O Allaah, show mercy to him."› [2]

---

1 Recorded by al-Bukhaaree, Muslim, and others from Aboo Hurayrah.
2 Recorded by al-Bukhaaree, Muslim, and others from Aboo Hurayrah.

The angels' prayer for the believers means that they ask Allaah to forgive them and show them mercy. As for Allaah's prayer for a person, as in the next *hadeeths*, it means that Allaah praises that person among the angels. With Allaah's praise, he is a greatly rewarded in the heavens and on earth.

Connecting the Rows in the Prayer. 'Aa'ishah (ﷺ) reported that the Prophet (ﷺ) said:

«إنّ الله تعالى وملائكتَهُ يُصلّونَ على الذينَ يصِلونَ الصفوفَ. ومن سدَّ فرجةً رفعه اللهُ بها درجةً.»

‹Indeed, Allaah (ﷻ) and His angels pray for those who connect the rows (in the prayer). Whoever fills a gap, Allaah raises him one level because of it.› [1]

Prayer in the First Row. In addition to going early to pray in the *masjid*, a Muslim is encouraged to stand in the front rows. The Prophet (ﷺ) said:

«إنّ اللهَ وملائِكَتَه يُصلّونَ على الصَّفِّ الأوّلِ (أو المُقدَّمِ).»

‹Indeed, Allaah and His angels pray for (those in) the front rows (in the prayer).› [2]

1 Recorded by Ahmad, Ibn Maajah, and others. Verified to be *hasan* (good) by al-Albaanee (*Saheeh ul-Jaami'* no. 1843 and *Saheeh ut-Targeeb* no. 501).

2 This *hadeeth* is recorded by Ahmad, Aboo Daawood, and others from

Going to Sleep with *Wudoo'*. Ibn 'Umar (ﷺ) reported that the Prophet (ﷺ) said:

«من باتَ طاهِراً باتَ في شِعارِهِ ملَكٌ، فلا يستيقِظُ ساعةً مِنَ الليلِ إلاّ قالَ المَلَكُ: "اللّهمّ اغْفِرْ لعبدِكَ فُلانٍ، فإنّه باتَ طاهِراً."»

‹When a person goes to sleep with *tahaarah* (or *wudoo'*), an angel stays in his covers. If he wakes up at any time of the night, the angel says, "O Allaah, forgive Your servant so-and-so because he slept with *tahaarah*."› [1]

Eating *Suhoor* (Early Breakfast) Before Fasting. Ibn 'Umar (ﷺ) reported that the Prophet (ﷺ) said:

«إنّ اللهَ وملائِكتَه يُصَلّونَ على الْمُتَسَحِّرِينَ.»

‹Indeed, Allaah and His angels pray for those who eat *suhoor*.› [2]

Visiting a Sick Muslim. 'Alee (ﷺ) reported that the Prophet (ﷺ) said:

---

al-Baraa', Aboo Umaamah, and other *sahaabah* (ﷺ). It is verified to be authentic by al-Albaanee (*Saheeh ul-Jaami'* nos. 1839-1842).

1 This *hadeeth* is recorded by Ibn Hibbaan and at-Tabaraanee. It is verified to be authentic by al-Albaanee (*as-Saheehah* no. 2539).

2 This *hadeeth* is recorded by Ibn Hibbaan, at-Tabaraanee, and others. It is verified to be *hasan* (good) by al-Albaanee (*Saheeh ul-Jaami'* no. 1844 and *as-Saheehah* no. 1654).

«ما من امرئ مسلم يعود مسلماً إلاّ ابتعث الله سبعينَ ألفَ ملكٍ يُصلّونَ عليه، في أيِّ ساعاتِ النهار كان، حتى يُمسي، وأيِّ ساعاتِ الليلِ كانَ، حتى يُصْبِحَ.»

‹Whenever a Muslim visits a sick Muslim, Allaah sends seventy thousand angels to pray for the visitor. If he visits him in the morning, they pray for him until the evening; and if he visits him in the evening, they pray for him until the morning.› [1]

Spending in Allaah's Way. There are angels who make *du'aa'* for those who spend money in the way of Allaah. This money goes for helping the poor, building *masjids*, teaching Islaam and Qur'aan, and so on. The Prophet (ﷺ) said:

«ما مِن يوم يُصبحُ فيه العِبادُ إلاّ ملكان ينزلان، فيقولُ أحدُهُما: "اللّهم أعطِ مُنفقاً خَلفاً." ويقولُ الآخرُ: اللّهمّ أعطِ مُمْسِكاً تلفاً.»

‹On the morning of every day, two angels descend (from the heavens). One of them says, "O Allaah, give more wealth to anyone who spends in Your way." And the other says, "O Allaah, destroy the wealth of anyone

1 Recorded by Ahmad and Ibn Hibbaan. Verified to be authentic by al-Albaanee (*as-Saheehah* no. 1367 and *Saheeh ul-Jaami'* no. 5687).

who refrains from spending (in Your way)."› [1]

Saying *Salaah* for the Prophet. 'Aamir Bin Rabee'ah (رضي الله عنه) reported that the Prophet (ﷺ) said:

«ما مِن عبدٍ يُصلِّي عليَّ إلاّ صلّتْ عليهِ الْملائكةُ،

ما دامَ يُصلّي عليَّ. فلْيُقِلَّ الْعبْدُ مِن ذلِك أو لِيُكْثِر.»

‹Whenever a person says *salaah* for me, the angels pray for him as long as he prays for me. Let him then choose whether to say little or much of this.› [2]

THEY SAY *AAMEEN* TO THE BELIEVERS' *DU'AA'*

When a Muslim makes *du'aa'* (supplication) for his Muslim brother, an angel says, "*Aameen.*" [3] The Prophet (ﷺ) said:

«دعوةُ الْمرءِ مُستَجابةٌ لأخيهِ بظَهْرِ الْغيبِ. عندَ رأسِهِ مَلَكٌ

يُؤَمِّنُ على دُعائِهِ، كُلّما دعا لهُ بخيرٍ قال: "آمين، ولكَ بمِثلِه."»

‹A Muslim's *du'aa'* for his brother in his absence is answered (by Allaah). There is an angel who remains present by his head, and

---

1 Recorded by al-Bukhaaree from Aboo Hurayrah (رضي الله عنه).

2 Recorded by Ahmad, Ibn Maajah, and others. Verified to be *hasan* (good) by al-Albaanee (*Saheeh ul-Jaami'* no. 5744).

3 "*Aameen*" means asking Allaah to accept the supplication.

whenever he asks good things for his brother, the angel says, "*Aameen*, and you be given the same."› [1]

Aboo Hurayrah (ﷺ) said that the Prophet (ﷺ) said:

«إذا قال الإمامُ: "آمين،" فإنّ الْملائكةَ تقولُ فِي السماءِ: "آمين." فإذا أمّنَ الإمامُ فأَمِّنوا، فإنّ مَن وافقَ تأمينُهُ تأمينَ الْملائِكةِ غُفِرَ لَهُ مَا تَقَدّمَ مِن ذَنبه.»

‹Surely, when the *imaam* (of the prayer) says "*aameen*," the angels in the heavens also say "*aameen*." So say "*aameen*" when the *imaam* says it. Indeed, whoever says "*aameen*" at the same time as the angels, his previous sins will be forgiven.› [2]

Umm Salamah (ﷺ) reported that the Prophet (ﷺ) said:

«إذا حضرتم المريض أو الميتَ فقولوا خيراً، فإن الملائكة يؤَمِّنونَ على ما تقولون.»

‹When you are present with a sick or dying person, say good things, because the angels say "*aameen*" to what you say.› [3]

1 Recorded by Muslim from Aboo ad-Dardaa' (ﷺ).
2 A combined report recorded by al-Bukhaaree, Muslim, and others.
3 Recorded by Muslim, al-Bayhaqee, and others.

THEY INTERCEDE FOR THE BELIEVERS

With Allaah's permission, the angels may intercede for the believers. Interceding means asking Allaah to forgive them and save them from the punishment. So it is a form of *du'aa'* or supplication. Allaah (ﷻ) says:

﴿وَكَم مِّن مَّلَكٍ فِي ٱلسَّمَـٰوَٰتِ لَا تُغْنِي شَفَـٰعَتُهُمْ شَيْـًٔا إِلَّا مِنۢ بَعْدِ أَن يَأْذَنَ ٱللَّهُ لِمَن يَشَآءُ وَيَرْضَىٰٓ ۝﴾ النجم ٢٦

«How many angels there are in the heavens whose intercession will be of no help except after Allaah has permitted and accepted it.» [1]

THEY STAY WITH THE BELIEVERS

The angels are with the believers all the time — except when the believers undress or go to toilet [2]. The Prophet (ﷺ) said:

«يتعاقبون فيكم، ملائكةٌ بالليل وملائكةٌ بالنهار، ويجتمعون في صلاةِ الفجرِ وصلاةِ العصرِ، ثم يعرجُ الذينَ باتوا فيكم، فيسألُهُم، وهو أعلمُ بهم: "كيف تركتُم عبادي؟" فيقولونَ: "تركناهُم وهُم يُصلّونَ، وأتيناهُم وهُم يُصلّون."»

1 *Soorat an-Najm* 53:26.
2 Except for the recording angels who never leave us.

‹There are two groups of angels who stay with you, one during the night and one during the day. They all meet at the *fajr* [1] and *'asr* [2] prayers. Those who have passed the night with you ascend to the heaven, and Allaah asks them, though He knows everything about them, "How did you leave my servants?" The angels reply, "When we left them, they were praying; also when we came to them, they were praying."› [3]

THEY HELP AND PROTECT THE BELIEVERS

The angels love the believers and protect them from *jinns*, Satan, disaster, and harm. Allaah says:

﴿لَهُۥ مُعَقِّبَـٰتٌ مِّنۢ بَيْنِ يَدَيْهِ وَمِنْ خَلْفِهِۦ يَحْفَظُونَهُۥ

مِنْ أَمْرِ ٱللَّهِ﴾ الرعد ١١

«(For each person) there are (angels) who follow each other. They stay before and behind him, guarding him by Allaah's decree.» [4]

Why do the angels protect the believers, and why do

1 This is the morning prayer that is made before the sunrise.

2 This is the afternoon prayer that is made before sunset.

3 Recorded by al-Bukhaaree, Muslim, and others from Aboo Hurayrah (ﷺ).

4 *Soorat ar-Ra'd* 13:11.

they stay with them? The answer is that a true believer always tries his best to obey Allaah and His Messenger (ﷺ) and do good deeds. He constantly remembers Allaah (ﷻ) with his tongue and in his heart. He remains aware of Allaah in all his actions. This is why the angels guard a believer and love him.

THEY LOVE AND HELP THE SEEKERS OF KNOWLEDGE

The angels love the knowledge of Islaam that brings a person closer to Allaah. They also love anyone who seeks to learn this important knowledge.

Safwaan Bin 'Assaal (رضي الله عنه) reported that he went to the Prophet (ﷺ) and told him that he came to seek knowledge of Islaam. The Prophet (ﷺ) said:

«مرحباً بطالب العلم. إنّ طالِبَ العِلمِ تَحُفُّه الْملائِكةُ وتظِلُّهُ بأجنِحتِها، ثم يركبُ بعضُهُم بعضاً حتى يبلغوا السماءَ الدنيا من مَحبَّتِهِم لِما يطلُب.»

‹Welcome, seeker of knowledge. Indeed, the angels surround a seeker of knowledge and shade him with their wings. Then they mount on top of each other up to the lowest heaven because they love what he seeks.› [1]

1 Recorded by Ahmad, Ibn Hibbaan, and others. Verified to be *hasan* by al-Albaanee (*Saheeh ut-Targheeb* no. 71).

Aboo ad-Dardaa' (ﷺ) reported that the Prophet (ﷺ) said:

«إنّ الْملائكةَ لتضعُ أجنِحَتَها لطالب العِلمِ رضاً بما يطلُب.»

‹Indeed, the angels lay down their wings for the seeker of knowledge because they are pleased with what he seeks.› [1]

The angels also pray for the teacher of the beneficial knowledge. Aboo Umaamah (ﷺ) reported that the Prophet (ﷺ) said:

«إنّ اللهَ وملائِكَتَه، حتى النملةَ فِي جُحْرِها، وحتى الحوتَ فِي البَحْرِ، ليُصَلّونَ على مُعَلِّمِ النّاسِ الخَيرَ.»

‹Indeed, Allaah, His angels, and even the ants in their hole and the fish in the sea, all pray for the teacher of goodness to people.› [2]

THEY TAKE CARE OF THE BELIEVERS AFTER DEATH

The angels take care of the righteous believers and martyrs after their death. They cover them with their wings, and they wash them if they need to be washed.

Jaabir Bin `Abdillaah (ﷺ) reported that when his father

1 Recorded by Aboo Daawood, at-Tirmithee, and others. Verified to be *hasan* by al-Albaanee (*Saheeh ut-Targheeb* no. 70 and *Saheeh ul-Jaami'* no. 1956).

2 Recorded by at-Tirmithee and at-Tabaraanee. Verified to be *hasan* by al-Albaanee (*Saheeh ut-Targheeb* no. 81 and *Saheeh ul-Jaami'* no. 1838).

died in the battle of Uhud, Jaabir's aunt Faatimah started weeping. The Prophet (ﷺ) told her:

«لا تبكي، ما زالت الملائكة تُظِله بأجنحتها حتى رفعتموه.»

‹Do not weep, because the angels continued shading him with their wings until he was raised (for burial).› [1]

Ibn 'Abbaas (رضي الله عنه) reported,

"Hamzah Bin 'Abd il-Muttalib and Hanzalah Bin ar-Raahib were both killed during the battle of Uhud, so Allaah's Messenger said, «رأيت الملائكة تغسِلُهما.» **‹I saw the angels washing them.›**" [2]

We will also see later in this chapter that the angels washed Aadam (عليه السلام) when he died.

They Fight on the Believers' Side

The angels fought in many battles on the side of the Muslims. For example, Allaah (سبحانه وتعالى) says about the battle of Badr:

1 Recorded by al-Bukaaree, Muslim, and others.

2 Recorded by at-Tabaraanee in *al-Kabeer* and Ibn Sa'd. Verified to be authentic by al-Albaanee (*Ahkaam ul-Janaa'iz* 75).

﴿إِذْ يُوحِي رَبُّكَ إِلَى ٱلْمَلَـٰٓئِكَةِ أَنِّي مَعَكُمْ فَثَبِّتُواْ ٱلَّذِينَ
ءَامَنُواْ ۚ سَأُلْقِي فِي قُلُوبِ ٱلَّذِينَ كَفَرُواْ ٱلرُّعْبَ فَٱضْرِبُواْ
فَوْقَ ٱلْأَعْنَاقِ وَٱضْرِبُواْ مِنْهُمْ كُلَّ بَنَانٍ ۝﴾ الأنفال ١٢

«(Remember) when your Lord told the angels, "Surely, I am with you, so help the believers. I will put fear in the hearts of the disbelievers. So hit (with your swords) over their necks, and on their fingers."» [1]

And the Prophet (ﷺ) said on that day:

«هذا جبريل آخذٌ برأسِ فرسِهِ، عليهِ أداةُ الْحَرْبِ.»

‹I see Jibreel holding the reins of his horse and ready with weapons for the battle.› [2]

THEY REMIND THE BELIEVERS OF DOING GOOD

The devils whisper to the people to do bad things. But the angels whisper to the believers to do good things. The Prophet (ﷺ) said:

«ما منكم من أحدٍ إلاّ وقد وُكِّل به قرينه من الجِنّ
وقرينه من الْملائكةِ.»

---

1 *Soorat al-Anfaal* 8:12.
2 Recorded by al-Bukhaaree from Ibn 'Abbaas (رضي الله عنه).

‹For each one of you is assigned a companion from the *jinn*s and a companion from the angels.›

The *sahaabah* asked the Prophet (ﷺ), "Do you too have a companion from the *jinn*s, O Allaah's Messenger?" He said:

«وإِيّايَ. ولكنّ اللهَ أعانني عليهِ فأسلمَ، فلا يأمُرُني إلاّ بخيرٍ.»

‹Yes, I too do. But Allaah has helped me to make him a Muslim. So he only tells me to do good things.› [1]

The Prophet (ﷺ) also said:

«إنّ للشيطان لَمّةً بابنِ آدمَ، ولِلمَلَكِ لَمّةً. فأمّا لَمّةُ الشيطانِ، فإيعادٌ بالشرِّ وتكذيبٌ بالْحقِّ. وأما لَمّةُ الْمَلَكِ، فإيعادٌ بالْخيرِ وتصديقٌ بالْحقِّ. فمن وجدَ ذلِك، فليعلمْ أنّه من اللهِ، فلْيحْمَدِ اللهَ. ومَن وجدَ الأُخرى، فلْيَتعوَّذْ باللهِ مِن الشيطانِ.»

‹A human being is touched by a devil and an angel. As for the devil's touch, it is that he calls to doing evil and denying the truth. And as for the angel's touch, it is that he calls to doing good and accepting the truth. When you feel this (the angel's touch), know that it is from Allaah and praise Allaah for it. And

1 Recorded by Muslim from Ibn Mas'ood (ﷺ).

when you feel the other touch, seek Allaah's protection from the Devil.› [1]

THEY TEACH THE BELIEVERS

Most of the good things that the people learnt from their prophets have been taught by the angels. Jibreel (ﷺ) taught the Qur'aan and many other things to the Prophet Muhammad (ﷺ).

The angels also taught us practical things to do in our life. For example, Ubayy Bin Ka'b (رضي الله عنه) reported that Allaah's Messenger (ﷺ) said:

«لما تُوفِّيَ آدمُ غسّلته الملائكةُ بالماء وتراً، وألحَدوا له،
وقالوا: هذه سنّةُ آدمَ في ولده.»

‹When Aadam died, the angels washed him with water an odd number of times, dug his grave, and said, "This will be a guidance for Aadam's descendants."› [2]

The Prophet (ﷺ) also tells us that the angels taught Aadam (عليه السلام) how to say *salaam* when he met other individuals. [3]

---

1 Recorded by Ahmad, at-Tirmithee, and others from Ibn Mas'ood (رضي الله عنه). Verified to be authentic by al-Albaanee (*al-Mishkaah* no. 70).

2 Recorded by al-Haakim and at-Tabaraanee. Verified to be authentic by al-Albaanee (*Saheeh ul-Jaami'* no. 5207).

3 Recorded by al-Bukhaaree and Muslim from Aboo Hurayrah.

THEY SPEAK UPON THE TONGUES OF THE BELIEVERS

The angels are Allaah's witnesses in the heavens. They also cause the righteous believers to say the right thing about a person — whether he is good or bad.

Anas (ﷺ) reported that the Prophet (ﷺ) said:

«الملائكة شُهداءُ الله في السماء، وأنتم شهداء الله في الأرض. إن لله ملائكةً تنطِقُ على ألسنةِ بني آدم بما في المرءِ من الخيرِ أو الشرّ.»

‹The angels are Allaah's witnesses in the heavens, and you (the believers) are Allaah's witnesses on earth. Indeed, Allaah has angels who speak upon the tongues of people telling what good or evil is in a person.› [1]

This means that the angels cause the righteous people to have a true opinion about others. For example, if the righteous people say that someone is good, most probably he is.

The Angels with the Prophets

Of all believers, the angels have a special love and respect for the prophets. They took Allaah's revelation to them, and

---

1 Recorded by al-Bukhaaree, Muslim, and others (*as-Saheehah* no. 1694).

they gave them advice and guidance.

In particular, we will see below that the angels do special things for our prophet Muhammad (ﷺ).

THEY SAY *SALAAH* UPON THE PROPHET

The angels say *salaah* upon the Prophet (ﷺ). This means that they make *du'aa'* for him. Allaah (ﷻ) says:

﴿إِنَّ ٱللَّهَ وَمَلَـٰٓئِكَتَهُۥ يُصَلُّونَ عَلَى ٱلنَّبِيِّ﴾ الأحزاب ٥٦

‹Surely, Allaah and His angels say *salaah* upon the Prophet.› [1]

THEY DELIVER *SALAAM* TO THE PROPHET

There are angels whose job is to receive the *salaah* and *salaam* that the Muslims say for the Prophet (ﷺ). They then take them to him in his grave. 'Abdullaah Bin Mas'ood (رضي الله عنه) reported that the Prophet (ﷺ) said:

«إنّ للهِ ملائكةً سياحينَ في الأرضِ يُبلّغوني عن أُمّتي السلامَ.»

‹Surely, Allaah has angels that travel over the earth and bring to me the *salaam* from my followers.› [2]

---

1 *Soorat al-Ahzaab* 33:56.

2 Recorded by Ahmad, an-Nasaa'ee, and others. Verified to be authentic by al-Albaanee (*Saheeh ul-Jaami'* no. 2174 and *al-Mishkaat* no. 884).

Aboo Bakr (ﷺ) reported that the Prophet (ﷺ) said:

«أكثِروا الصلاةَ عليَّ، فإنّ اللهَ وكّلَ بي ملَكاً عِندَ قبري، فإذا صلّى عليَّ رجلٌ من أمّتي قال لي ذلكَ الْمَلَكُ: "يا مُحَمّدُ، إنّ فُلانَ بنَ فُلانٍ صلّى عليكَ الساعةَ."»

‹Say *salaah* for me in plenty. Indeed, Allaah has appointed an angel by my grave. When one of my followers says *salaah* for me, the angel says, "O Muhammad, so-and-so has just said *salaah* for you."› [1]

THEY PROTECTED THE PROPHET FROM HARM

The evil disbeliever Aboo Jahl once wanted to harm the Prophet (ﷺ). He said, "Surely, if I see Muhammad praying at the Ka'abah, I will step on his neck." But when he tried doing this, he was scared by great fires and wings that he saw in front of him. When the Prophet (ﷺ) heard of this, he said:

«لو دنا مِنّي لاخْتَطَفَتْهُ الْمَلائِكَةُ عُضْواً عُضْواً.»

‹If he came any closer, the angels would surely have torn him to pieces.› [2]

1 Recorded by ad-Daylamee, at-Tabaraanee, and others. Verified to be *hasan* by al-Albaanee (*as-Saheehah* no. 1530).

2 Recorded by al-Bukhaaree and Muslim from Ibn 'Abbaas (ﷺ).

There is an angel whom Allaah has made in charge of the mountains. He was ready to destroy the disbelievers who harmed the Prophet (ﷺ). 'Aa'ishah (رضي الله عنها) reported that the Prophet (ﷺ) said:

«لقد لقِيتُ مِن قَوْمِكِ ما لَقِيتُ، وكَانَ أشَدُّ ما لَقِيتُ مِنهُم يومَ العَقَبَةِ. فَٱنطلقتُ وأنا مَهمومٌ على وَجْهي، فَلَم أستَفِقْ إلاّ وأنا بقرنِ الثَّعالِب، فرفعْتُ رأسي، فإذا أنا بسحابةٍ قد أظَلَّتني، فنظَرتُ فإذا فيها جِبريلُ، فنَاداني فقال: "إنّ اللهَ قَدْ سَمعَ قولَ قَوْمِكَ لَكَ وما رَدُّوا بهِ عليك، وقدْ بعَثَ إلِيْكَ مَلَكَ الْجِبالِ لِتَأْمُرَه بما شِئْتَ فيهم." فناداني مَلَكُ الْجِبالِ فسَلَّمَ عليَّ، ثُمَّ قال: "يا مُحَمَّد، فما شِئْتَ. إن شِئْتَ أن أُطْبِقَ عليهِم الأخشَبين." قلتُ: "بلْ أرجُو أن يُخْرِجَ اللهُ مِن أصلابِهِم مَن يعبُدُ" اللهَ لا يُشْرِكُ بِهِ شَيْئاً.»

‹I have suffered so much harm from your people (the Quraysh). The hardest was during the Day of 'Aqabah [1]. I became so depressed that I walked for a long time without paying attention to anything. Finally, I found myself at Qarn ath-Tha'aalib. A cloud covered me, and I looked up to see Jibreel in it. He said,

1 'Aqabah is on the west edge of Makkah at the border of Minaa.

"Indeed, Allaah has heard what your people said and did to you. He has sent to you the Angel of Mountains so you would tell him what you want him to do to them." The Angel of the Mountains then called me, said *Salaam*, and said, "O Muhammad! If you wish, I will make these two great mountains (of Makkah) fall on top of them." I said, "No! I hope that Allaah will bring from their children those who worship Allaah alone."› [1]

The Angels with the Sinners and Disbelievers

The angels hate those who disbelieve in Allaah (ﷻ) and do things that displease Him. They hate sins and sometimes curse those who commit them.

They Curse the Disbelievers

The angels curse the *kuffaar* because they do not believe in Allaah and they do bad things. Allaah (ﷻ) says:

﴿إِنَّ ٱلَّذِينَ كَفَرُواْ وَمَاتُواْ وَهُمْ كُفَّارٌ أُوْلَـٰٓئِكَ عَلَيْهِمْ لَعْنَةُ
ٱللَّهِ وَٱلْمَلَـٰٓئِكَةِ وَٱلنَّاسِ أَجْمَعِينَ ۝﴾ البقرة ١٦١

«Surely, those who disbelieve in Allaah and die as *kuffaar*, on them is the curse of Allaah,

1 Recorded by al-Bukhaaree, Muslim, and others.

the angels, and all the people.» [1]

THEY PUNISH THE DISBELIEVERS

Sometimes, the angels bring down Allaah's punishment and anger over the disbelievers and wrongdoers. As an example, we saw earlier [2] that the angels who came to Ibraaheem were also sent to punish the people of Loot. Allaah (ﷻ) punished those people by making the angels drop down upon them poisonous stones from Hell.

THEY STAY AWAY FROM SINNERS

A sinner loses the company of angels and gains the company of devils. He can only change this by quickly repenting to Allaah (ﷻ).

Ibn 'Abbaas (ﷺ) reported that the Prophet (ﷺ) said:

«ثلاثةٌ لا تقرَبُهمُ الملائكةُ: الجُنُبُ، والسِّكرانُ، والمتضمِّخُ بالخَلوق.»

‹There are three individuals whom the angels do not approach: a *junub*, a drunk person, and a man who wears *khalooq*.› [3]

---

1 *Soorat al-Baqarah* 2:161-162.

2 In Chapter 2.

3 Recorded by al-Bazzaar and al-Bukhaaree (in *at-Taareekh*). Verified to be authentic by al-Albaanee (*as-Saheehah* no. 1804).

A *junub* is a person who is in a state of major impurity or uncleanliness requiring *ghusl* (bath). It is prohibited to remain *junub* for a long time, because this would prevent from prayer and from remembering Allaah.

Khalooq is a women's perfume that contains saffron. It is prohibited for men to wear it.

Other Things the Angels Do

THEY CONDUCT ALL AFFAIRS

Allaah (ﷻ) can do everything by Himself. Things can happen immediately by Allaah's command. But Allaah's great wisdom has dictated that things in this world happen through some means. And the angels are among the means for doing most things. Allaah chooses for angels to bring down His revelation, record our deeds, take our souls, manage the rain, plants, and food, and so on.

Allaah (ﷻ) describes the angels as:

﴿فَٱلْمُدَبِّرَاتِ أَمْرًا ۝﴾ النازعات ٥

«And those (angels) who arrange all matters (according to Allaah's orders).» [1]

1 *Soorat an-Naazi'aat* 79:5.

He (ﷻ) also says:

﴿فَٱلْمُقَسِّمَـٰتِ أَمْرًا ۝﴾ الذاريات ٤

«And those (angels) who distribute all things (according to Allaah's orders).» [1]

As an example, the Prophet (ﷺ) tells us that thunder is actually the sound of an angel who praises Allaah and manages the clouds. Ibn 'Abbaas (رضي الله عنه) reported that the Prophet (ﷺ) said:

«الرعدُ مَلَكٌ من ملائِكةِ اللهِ، مُوَكّلٌ بالسَّحاب، معهُ مَخاريقُ من نارٍ، يسوقُ بها السَّحابَ حيثُ شاءَ اللهُ.»

‹Thunder is one of Allaah's Angels. He is in charge of the clouds, and he has spears of fire that he uses for driving the clouds wherever Allaah wills.› [2]

They Protect the Sacred Places

The angels protect the three sacred cities: Makkah, al-Madeenah, and Jerusalem. The Prophet (ﷺ) said:

«على أنقابِ الْمدينةِ ملائكةٌ، لا يدخُلُها الطاعونُ ولا الدجَّالُ.»

---

1 *Soorat ath-Thaariyaat* 51:4.

2 Recorded by Ahmad, at-Tirmithee, and others. Verified to be authentic by al-Albaanee (*as-Saheehah* no. 1872 and *Saheeh ul-Jaami'* no. 3553).

‹There are angels around the corners of al-Madeenah, so that plague and ad-Dajjaal (the Great Liar) may not enter it.› [1]

And the Prophet (ﷺ) said:

«ليس من بلدٍ إلا سيطؤه الدجّالُ، إلاّ مكّةَ والْمدينةَ، ليس له من نِقابها نَقْبٌ إلاّ عليه الْملائكةُ صافّينَ يحرُسونَها.»

‹Every town will be entered by ad-Dajjaal, except for Makkah and al-Madeenah. There are angels lined up to guard every corner around them.› [2]

And he (ﷺ) said:

«طوبى للشامِ، تلك ملائِكةُ اللهِ باسطو أجنِحتِها على الشامِ.»

‹Glad news for Shaam (Jerusalem and the surrounding lands). Here are Allaah's angels spreading their wings over Shaam.› [3]

1 Recorded by al-Bukhaaree from Aboo Hurayrah (رضي الله عنه).
2 Recorded by al-Bukhaaree and Muslim from Anas (رضي الله عنه).
3 Recorded by at-Tirmithee, al-Haakim, and others from Zayd Bin Thaabit (رضي الله عنه). Verified to be authentic by al-Albaanee (*as-Saheehah* no. 503 and *Saheeh ul-Jaami'* no. 3920).

Questions and Exercises

1. In the following table, check all true statements (23 points):

	Statement	✓
a	The angels worship Allaah all the time.	
b	The angels do not fear Allaah because they know Him.	
c	Jesus is an obedient servant to Allaah.	
d	The angels cannot obey Allaah all the time.	
e	The heavens are completely filled with angels.	
f	The angels descend to earth during their free time.	
g	The angels are close to Allaah.	
h	The angels love whatever they want.	
i	The angels form straight lines before Allaah.	
j	The angels say *salaah* upon the Prophet.	
k	The angels stay with the believers all the time.	
l	The angels make *hajj* (pilgrimage).	
m	The angels write what the believers do, and the *jinns* write what the disbelievers do.	

	Statement	✓
n	The angels convey Allaah's messages to the people.	
o	"Cupid" is a friendly angel.	
p	The angels would never harm anyone.	
q	Al-Bayt ul-Ma'moor to the angels is like al-Ka'bah to us.	
r	Allaah sends an angel to give us life.	
s	When we reach puberty, an angels writes our future.	
t	The angels say *aameen* before the *imaam*.	
u	There is an additional reward for making *du'aa'* for a Muslim in his absence.	
v	It is not important to sleep with *tahaarah*.	
w	The angels protect the sacred places.	

2. Mention three acts of worship the angels do (6 points):

1	3
2	

3. The best *thikr* is (2 points):

4. Check all true statements regarding the angels who record our deeds (5 points):

	Statement	✓
a	There are two of them on each side of us.	
b	They are honorable and precise.	
c	They do not know what we do secretly.	
d	Each of them records our good and bad deeds.	
e	They give us a chance to repent from our sins.	

5. Mention five things that the angels ask Allaah to give to the believers, as in the beginning of *Soorat Ghaafir* (10 points):

1	4
2	5
3	

6. Mention eight situations where the angels supplicate for the believers (8 points):

1	5
2	6
3	7
4	8

7. Mention ten things the angels do that reflect their love for the believers (10 points):

1	6
2	7
3	8
4	9
5	10

8. Mention three things the angels do that show their love for the Prophet (ﷺ) (3 points):

1	3
2	

9. Mention three things that the angels do to the *kuffaar* and other wrongdoers (3 points):

1	3
2	

10. Explain how the angels coduct all affairs (3 points):

CHAPTER 4

ANGELS THAT WE KNOW

In this chapter, we introduce specific angels that have been mentioned in the Qur'aan or Sunnah, and we highlight some important things that we know about them.

Jibreel

The most important angel is Jibreel (ﷺ). He is respected and obeyed by all other angels. Allaah (ﷻ) says about him:

﴿إِنَّهُۥ لَقَوْلُ رَسُولٍ كَرِيمٍ ۝ ذِي قُوَّةٍ عِندَ ذِي ٱلْعَرْشِ مَكِينٍ ۝ مُّطَاعٍ ثَمَّ أَمِينٍ ۝﴾ التكوير ١٩-٢١

«This (Qur'aan) is surely a Word brought by a noble Messenger (Jibreel). He is powerful, and has a high position with the Lord of the Throne (Allaah). He is obeyed (in the heavens) and is trustworthy.» [1]

Names of Jibreel

The English word for Jibreel is Gabriel. Jibreel is mentioned

---

1 *Soorat at-Takweer* 81:19-21.

many times in the Qur'aan, sometimes by name and sometimes by description.

Jibreel (عليه السلام) is called in the Qur'aan "ar-Rooh" which means "the Spirit" or "the Life". The reason for this name is that Jibreel (عليه السلام) is the angel who carried the teachings from Allaah (سبحانه وتعالى) to the Prophets. These teachings gave life and spirit to the hearts of many people.

Jibreel (عليه السلام) was also chosen to blow the life of the noble prophet 'Eesaa (عليه السلام) into the body of his mother Maryam. He breathed into an opening in her clothes. The breath traveled into her body, and she became pregnant with 'Eesaa (عليه السلام).

Jibreel (عليه السلام) is also called "ar-Rooh ul-Ameen" which means "the Trustworthy Spirit". Allaah (سبحانه وتعالى) says:

﴿وَإِنَّهُ لَتَنزِيلُ رَبِّ ٱلْعَـٰلَمِينَ ۝ نَزَلَ بِهِ ٱلرُّوحُ ٱلْأَمِينُ ۝
عَلَىٰ قَلْبِكَ لِتَكُونَ مِنَ ٱلْمُنذِرِينَ ۝﴾ الشعراء ١٩٢-١٩٤

«And truly, this (Qur'aan) is sent down from the Lord of the worlds. The Trustworthy Spirit has brought it down upon your heart (O Muhammad), so that you may be of the warners.» [1]

Allaah gave Jibreel the most important responsibility of delivering His messages to the human messengers.

Jibreel (عليه السلام) is also called "Rooh ul-Qudus", which means "the Spirit that Belongs to the Holy One". "The Holy

---

1 *Soorat ash-Shu'araa'* 26:192-194.

One" or "al-Qudus" is Allaah (ﷻ). Allaah also called Jibreel "Roohunaa", which means, "the Spirit that Belongs to Us".

THE FIRST MEETING WITH THE PROPHET

The Prophet Muhammad (ﷺ) saw Jibreel for the first time in Makkah. The Prophet (ﷺ) was sitting alone at the entrance of a small cave on a mountainside when he saw him up in the sky. Jibreel then came down until he was very close to the Prophet (ﷺ). Allaah (ﷻ) says:

﴿فَكَانَ قَابَ قَوْسَيْنِ أَوْ أَدْنَىٰ ۝ فَأَوْحَىٰ إِلَىٰ عَبْدِهِ مَا أَوْحَىٰ ۝﴾ النجم ٩-١٠

«And he (Jibreel) was at a distance of two bow lengths or nearer. And He (Allaah) revealed to His servant (Muhammad) what He revealed.» [1]

'Aa'ishah (رضي الله عنها) said that the Prophet (ﷺ) told her:

«رأيت جبريل عليه السلام على صورته التي خُلق عليها مرتين: مرةً عندَ سِدرةِ الْمُنتَهى، ومرّةً في أجيادَ، رأيتُه

1 *Soorat an-Najm* 53:8-9.

مُنهَبطًا من السماء، له ستُّمِائَةِ جناح، ساداً عِظَمُ خَلْقِه الأفقَ ما بين السماء إلى الأرض.»

‹I saw Jibreel (ﷺ) twice in his actual form in which Allaah created him: once at Sidrat ul-Muntahaa (the fern tree at the Throne), and once in Ajyaad [1]. I saw him flying down from the heaven, having six-hundred wings, and his huge size covered all space from the heaven to earth.› [2]

Ibn Mas'ood (ﷺ) reported that the Prophet (ﷺ) said:

«أتاني جبريل في خَضِرٍ معلّقٍ به الدُّرّ.»

‹Jibreel came to me wearing green silk garments with pearls attached to them.› [3]

'Abdullaah Bin Mas'ood (ﷺ) also reported:

"رأى رسولُ اللهِ رَفْرَفًا أَخضرَ سدَّ أُفُقَ السّماءِ.

رأى جبريل، له ستُّمائَةِ جناحٍ."

"Allaah's Messenger (ﷺ) saw a green screen covering the horizon. He saw Jibreel with

1 A place in Makkah.

2 This is a combined report from al-Bukhaaree, Muslim, and others.

3 Recorded by Ahmad and ad-Daaraqutnee. Verified to be authentic by al-Albaanee (*as-Saheehah* no. 3485).

six-hundred wings." [1]

Of course, when Jibreel took a human form, he did not have the wings, nor did he come in that large size. Rather, he resembled a handsome *sahaabee* called Duhyah al-Kalbee. 'Aa'ishah (ﷺ) reported that the Prophet (ﷺ) said:

«أشبهُ ما رأيتُ بِجبريلَ دُحيةُ الكلبيّ.»

‹The person that I have seen most similar to Jibreel is Duhyah al-Kalbee.› [2]

COMPANION DURING *ISRAA'* AND *MI'RAAJ*

Jibreel accompanied the Prophet (ﷺ) on his night journey from Makkah to Jerusalem. That journey is called *al-Israa'*. During the same night, he also went up with the Prophet (ﷺ) on a journey to the heavens. That journey is called *al-Mi'raaj*.

The story of *al-Mi'raaj* is told by Anas Bin Maalik (ﷺ). He said that Allaah's Messenger (ﷺ) said:

«فُرِجَ عن سقفِ بيتي بمَكّةَ، فنزَلَ جبريل، ففَرَجَ صَدْري،

ثمَّ غسَلَه بِماءِ زمزَمَ، ثمّ جاء بطَستٍ من ذهب مُمْتلِئٍ حِكْمةً

---

1 Recorded by al-Bukhaaree, Muslim, and others.

2 Recorded by Ibn Sa'd. Verified to be authentic by al-Albaanee (*as-Saheehah* no. 1111). Another *hadeeth* with a similar meaning is recorded by Muslim and others from Jaabir (ﷺ).

وإيمانًا، فأفرَغه في صدري ثُمَّ أَطبَقه.»

‹While I was at Makkah, the roof of my house opened and Jibreel descended. He opened my chest and washed it with Zamzam water. Then he brought a golden bowl full of wisdom and faith, poured its contents into my chest, and closed it.›

The Prophet (ﷺ) then described the *Israa'* from Makkah to Jerusalem. Then he continued:

«ثمّ أخَذَ بيدِي فعرَجَ بي إلى السّماءِ الدّنيا. قال جبريلُ لِخازنِ السّماءِ: "اْفتَح." قال: "مَن هذا؟" قال: "هذا جبريلُ." قال: "هل معَكَ أحدٌ؟" قال: "نعم، معِيَ مُحَمّدٌ." قالَ: "أُرسِلَ إليهِ؟" قال: "نعم." ففتَحَ. فلمّا فتَحَ علونا السّماءَ الدُّنيا.»

‹He took my hand and ascended with me. When we reached the lowest heaven, Jibreel said to its gatekeeper, "Open the gate." The angel asked, "Who is it?" Jibreel answered, "This is Jibreel." He asked him, "Is there anyone with you?" Jibreel replied, "Yes, Muhammad (ﷺ) is with me." He asked him, "Has he been summoned?" Jibreel replied, "Yes." So the gate was opened, and we went

up into the lowest heaven.› [1]

This *hadeeth* continues to tell the story of the trip of the Prophet (ﷺ) with Jibreel all the way up to the highest heaven. Jibreel then showed him *Jannah*:

«ثُمَ أُدخِلتُ الْجَنّةَ، فإذا فيها حَبائِلُ اللؤْلؤ، وإذا تُرابُها الْمِسكُ.»

‹I was then admitted into *Jannah.* I saw in it tents made of pearls, and I found that its soil is made of musk."› [2]

The full story of *al-Israa'* and *al-Mi'raaj* is long, and we hope to have it in a separate book, *in-shaa' Allaah.*

TEACHING QUR'AAN TO THE PROPHET

Jibreel (عليه السلام) brought the Qur'aan from Allaah (سبحانه وتعالى) to the Prophet (ﷺ). He taught the Prophet (ﷺ) how to read it and understand it. Faatimah (رضي الله عنها) said that her father, the Prophet (ﷺ), told her shortly before he died:

«إنّ جبريلَ كان يُعارِضُني القرآنَ كل سنةٍ مرةً، وإنّه عارَضَنِي
العامَ مرّتينِ، ولا أراهُ إلاّ حضرَ أجلي، وإنّكِ أولُ أهلِ بيتي

1 Recorded by al-Bukhaaree.
2 Recorded by al-Bukhaaree, Muslim, and others.

لُحوقاً بي، فاتّقي اللهَ واْصبري، فإنّي نعمَ السلفُ أنا لكِ.»

‹Indeed, Jibreel used to check my knowledge of the Qur'aan once every year. But indeed, he has done this twice this year. I only see this as a sign that my time (of death) has come. And indeed, you are the first member of my household to follow me. So fear Allaah and be patient. Indeed, I am the best role-model for you.› [1]

Jibreel usually taught the Qur'aan to the Prophet (ﷺ) during the month of *Ramadhaan*. Ibn 'Abbaas (رضي الله عنهما) said:

"كان رسول اللهِ أجودَ الناسِ. وكانَ أجودَ ما يكونُ
فِي رمضانَ حين يأتيهِ جبريلُ فيُدارسُهُ القرآن
فلرسولُ اللهِ أجودُ بالْخَيرِ من الريحِ الْمُرسلةِ."

"The Messenger of Allaah (ﷺ) was the most generous person. And he was most generous during *Ramadhaan* when Jibreel came to him to teach him the Qur'aan. Surely, the Messenger of Allaah was then more generous than free wind." [2]

---

1 Recorded by al-Bukhaaree, Muslim, and others. The last sentence is not in al-Bukhaaree or Muslim, but is verified to be authentic by al-Albaanee (*as-Saheehah* no. 3524).

2 Recorded by al-Bukhaaree and others.

TEACHING THE PROPHET AND THE MUSLIMS

Jibreel (ﷺ) gave much advice to the Prophet (ﷺ) and taught him many important things. We have seen how he visited the *Masjid* of the Prophet (ﷺ) and taught the Muslims about Islaam, *Eemaan*, and *Ihsaan* [1].

In another example, 'Aa'ishah said that the Prophet (ﷺ) said:

«ما زالَ جبريلُ يوصيني بالجارِ حتى ظننتُ أنّه سيورِّثه.»

‹Jibreel kept telling me to be kind to the neighbors until I thought that he would tell me to give them of the inheritance [2].› [3]

Jibreel taught the Prophet (ﷺ) how to perform *wudoo'* and prayer. The Prophet (ﷺ) said:

«أتاني جبريلُ في أوّلِ ما أوحِيَ إليّ، فعلّمني الوضوءَ والصّلاةَ.»

‹In the beginning of my message, Jibreel came to me and taught me how to perform *wudoo'* and *salaah*.› [4]

The Prophet (ﷺ) also tells us that Jibreel taught him how and when to perform the five prayers:

---

1 Review Part 1 (Knowing Allaah) of this series.
2 Money left by a person after death.
3 Recorded by al-Bukhaaree, Muslim, and others.
4 Recorded by Ibn Maajah, Ahmad, and others, from Zayd Bin Haarithah (ﷺ). Verified to be authentic by al-Albaanee (*as-Saheehah* no. 841).

«نزلَ جبريلُ، فأمّني فصلّيتُ معه، ثم صلّيتُ معه،

ثم صلّيتُ معه، ثم صلّيتُ معه، ثم صلّيتُ معه.»

‹Jibreel descended and led me in the prayer. I prayed with him, then I prayed with him (the next prayer), then I prayed with him, then I prayed with him, then I prayed with him.› [1]

Jibreel and Meekaa'eel also taught the Prophet (ﷺ) how to read the Qur'aan in seven different ways. [2]

SUPPLICATING FOR THE PROPHET

Jibreel (عليه السلام) taught the Prophet (ﷺ) many *du'aa*'s and *athkaar* for protection from harm. For example, Aboo Sa'eed al-Khudree (رضي الله عنه) reported that once Jibreel visited the Prophet (ﷺ) and asked him, "O Muhammad, are you sick?" He replied, «نعم.» **‹Yes.›** Jibreel then said:

«بسم الله أرقيك، من كل شيء يؤذيك، من شر كل

نفسٍ أو عين حاسد، الله يشفيك، بسم الله أرقيك.»

‹Bismillaahi arqeek, min kulli shay'in

---

1 Recorded by al-Bukhaaree, Muslim, and others from Aboo Mas'ood (رضي الله عنه).

2 Recorded by an-Nasaa'ee, Ahmad, and others, from Ubayy Bin Ka'b (رضي الله عنه). Verified to be authentic by al-Albaanee (*as-Saheehah* no. 841).

***yu'theek, min sharri kulli nafsin aw 'ayni haasid; Allaah yashfeek; bismillaahi arqeek* — With Allaah's Name I shelter you, from all that ails you, from the evil of any soul, and that of the envious eye. May Allaah cure you; with Allaah's Name I shelter you.›** [1]

SAYING *SALAAM* TO THE PROPHET'S WIVES

Jibreel (ﷺ) would often ask the Prophet (ﷺ) to give *salaam* to his wives. For example, the Prophet (ﷺ) said that Jibreel told him:

«"يا محمد، أقرأ على خديجة من ربها السلامَ."»

‹O Muhammad, give *salaam* to Khadeejah from her Lord.› [2]

Similarly, 'Aa'ishah (ﷺ) reported that on a number of occasions, the Prophet (ﷺ) would say to her:

«يا عائشة، هذا جبريل يُقرِئُكِ السلام.»

‹O 'Aa'ishah, Jibreel is here, and he gives you *salaam*.› [3]

1 Recorded by Muslim and others.
2 Recorded by al-Bukhaaree, Muslim, and others from Aboo Hurayrah.
3 Recorded by al-Bukhaaree, Muslim, and others.

Meekaa'eel

Meekaa'eel is one of the nearest angels to Allaah. Some of the scholars believe that his jobs include bringing rain, plants, and food to the creation (all by Allaah's permission). We must love him and all the angels, as Allaah (ﷻ) says:

﴿مَن كَانَ عَدُوًّا لِلّهِ وَمَلَـٰٓئِكَتِهِۦ وَرُسُلِهِۦ وَجِبْرِيلَ وَمِيكَىٰلَ فَإِنَّ ٱللَّهَ عَدُوٌّ لِّلْكَـٰفِرِينَ ۝﴾ البقرة ٩٨

«Whoever is an enemy of Allaah, His angels, His messengers, Jibreel, and Meekaal: surely, Allaah is an enemy to the disbelievers.» [1]

Meekaa'eel stopped smiling when Allaah (ﷻ) created Hell. The Prophet (ﷺ) said:

«قلتُ لِجبريل: "مالي لم أرَ ميكائيلَ ضاحكاً قطُّ؟"

قال: "ما ضحِكَ ميكائيلُ منذُ خُلقتِ النارُ."»

‹I asked Jibreel, "Why have I never seen Meekaa'eel smile?" Jibreel replied, "Meekaa'eel never smiled since the Fire was created."› [2]

1 *Soorat al-Baqarah* 2:98.

2 Verified to be *hasan* (good) by al-Albaanee (*as-Saheehah* no. 2511).

Israafeel and the Horn Blower

Israafeel (ﷺ) is not mentioned in the Qur'aan, but is mentioned in the following *du'aa'* that the Prophet (ﷺ) sometimes said when he started his night prayers:

«اللهُمَّ ربَّ جِبريلَ وميكائيلَ وإسرافيلَ، فاطِرَ السَّماواتِ والأرضِ، عـالمَ الغَيبِ والشَّـهادةِ، أنتَ تحكُم بينَ عِبادِكَ فيما كانوا فيه يختلِفُونَ، اهْدِني لِما اختُلِفَ فيه منَ الحقِّ بـإذْنِـكَ، إنَّـكَ تَـهْدِي مَنْ تَشَاءُ إلى صِراطٍ مُسْتَقِيم»

‹*Allaahumma rabba jibreela wa-meekaa'eela wa-israafeel, faatir as-samaawaati wal-ard, 'aalim al-ghaybi wash-shahaadah, anta tahkumu bayna 'ibaadika feemaa kaanoo feehi yakhtalifoon. Ihdinee li-ma-khtulifa feehi min al-haqqi bi-ithnika, innaka tahdee man tashaa'u ilaa siraatin mustaqeem* —
Oh Allaah! You are the Lord of Jibreel, Meekaa'eel, and Israafeel. You are the Creator of the heavens and earth. You know all about what we cannot see and what we can see. You judge among Your servants when they disagree. So guide me, by Your permission, to the truth when the people differ. You truly guide whom You will to the Straight Path.› [1]

1 Recorded by Muslim from 'Aa'ishah (ﷺ).

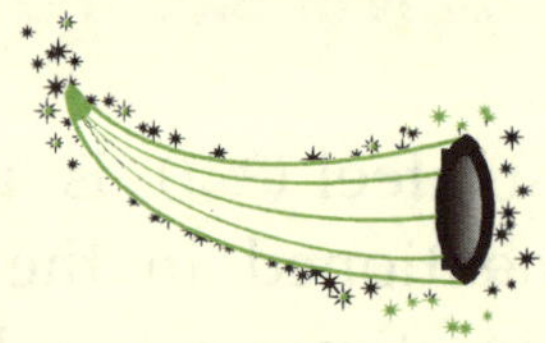

When Allaah wants to end the life in this world, a horn will be blown. Everyone will then die except for those whom Allaah wants to keep alive. The horn will be blown again, and everyone will rise from death. Allaah (ﷻ) says:

﴿وَنُفِخَ فِي ٱلصُّورِ فَصَعِقَ مَن فِي ٱلسَّمَٰوَٰتِ وَمَن فِي ٱلْأَرْضِ، إِلَّا مَن
شَآءَ ٱللَّهُ، ثُمَّ نُفِخَ فِيهِ أُخْرَىٰ فَإِذَا هُمْ قِيَامٌ يَنظُرُونَ ۝﴾ الزمر ٦٨

«And the Horn will be blown. All who are in the heavens and on earth will fall dead, except those whom Allaah will spare. Then it will be blown again, and at once they will all be standing and looking around them.» [1]

This Horn will be blown by an angel whom Allaah appointed for this job. The Prophet (ﷺ) said:

«إنّ طرفَ صاحِبِ الصّور منذُ وُكِل به مُستعِدٌّ، ينظرُ نحوَ العرشِ،
مَخافةَ أن يُؤمَرَ قبلَ أن يرتَدَّ إليهِ طرفُه، كأن عينيهِ كوكبانِ دُرّيان.»

‹Indeed, the eyesight of the holder of the Horn is ever-ready since he was given charge of it. He looks steadily toward the Throne, fearing (if he blinks) that the command will come before his glance returns to him. His

1 *Soorat az-Zumar* 39:68.

eyes are like two bright planets.› [1]

Similarly, Aboo Sa'eed al-Khudree and a number of other *sahaabah* (رضي الله عنهم) reported that the Prophet (ﷺ) said:

«كيفَ أنعَمُ وقد ٱلتقَمَ صاحِبُ القَرْنِ القرنَ، وحَنَّى جبهَتَه،
وأصغى سمعَه، ينتظِرُ أن يُؤمرَ أن ينفُخَ فينفُخ.»

‹How can I feel secure when the holder of the Horn has placed the Horn against his mouth and has bent his forehead. He listens carefully, awaiting the command to blow so as to blow it.› [2]

There is no authentic *hadeeth* giving the name of the Horn Blower, but most *'ulamaa'* believe that it is Israafeel (عليه السلام).

The Angel of Death and His Helpers

The Angel of Death

Allaah has given some of the angels the job of taking the lives of people. The chief of these angles is known as the Angel of Death. Allaah (سبحانه وتعالى) says about him:

1 Recorded by al-Haakim from Aboo Hurayrah (رضي الله عنه). Verified to be authentic by al-Albaanee (*as-Saheehah* no. 1078).

2 Recorded by Ahamd, at-Tirmithee, and others. Verified to be authentic by al-Albaanee (*as-Saheehah* no. 1079).

﴿قُلْ يَتَوَفَّاكُم مَّلَكُ ٱلْمَوْتِ ٱلَّذِي وُكِّلَ بِكُمْ ثُمَّ إِلَىٰ رَبِّكُمْ تُرْجَعُونَ﴾ السجدة ١١

«Tell them (O Muhammad), "The Angel of Death, who is assigned to you, will take away your lives. Then you will be brought before your Lord." » [1]

Some people call the Angel of Death "'Izraa'eel". As we indicated earlier [2], it is wrong to use this name because it is not mentioned in the Qur'aan or Sunnah.

THE ANGEL OF DEATH WITH MOOSAA

In the early times, the Angel of Death sometimes came to humans in the form of a man. This happened to the noble prophet Moosaa (ﷺ). When the angel came to take away his life, Moosaa did not recognize him at first. When he told him, "Get ready to die," Moosaa thought that he was an evil person trying to harm him, so he punched him in the eye [3]. The Prophet (ﷺ) said:

«إنّ ملَكَ المْوتِ كان يأتي الناسَ عَياناً، حتى أتى موسى بنَ عِمرانَ، فقال له: "أجِبْ ربّك." فلطَمَ موسى عينَ

1 *Soorat as-Sajdah* 32:11.
2 In Chapter 1.
3 This is explained very well by al-Albaanee (رحمه الله) in *as-Saheehah* vol. 7, pp. 826-835.

ملكِ الْموتِ ففقأها.»

‹The Angel of Death used to come to (some) people in a visible way (i.e., in the form of a man). So, he came to Moosaa (ﷺ) and said to him, "Come to your Lord." On hearing this, Moosaa punched him and knocked out his eye.›

«فرجعَ الْمَلَكُ إلَى اللهِ، فقال: " يا ربِّ، إنّكَ أرسَلْتَني إلَى عبدٍ لَكَ لا يُريدُ الْموتَ، وقد فقأَ عيني. ولولا كرامَتَه عليكَ لشقَقتُ عليه."»

‹The angel went back to Allaah and said, "My Lord, You sent me to a person who does not wish to die. Indeed, he has knocked out my eye. If he did not have a noble position with You, I would have dealt with him harshly."›

«فردَّ اللهُ إليهِ عينَه، وقال: "ارجِع إلى عبدي فقُل: الْحياةَ تُريدُ؟ فإن كُنتَ تريدُ الْحياةَ فضع يدَكَ على متنِ ثور، فما توارَت يَدُك من شعرةٍ فإنّك تعيشُ بها سنةً."»

‹So Allaah restored his eye and said, "Go back to my servant and ask him if he wishes to live longer. If he does, then tell him to put

his hand on the back of an Ox. For every hair that his hand touches, he will have a year to live."›

«قال: "أي ربِّ، ثُمّ مَه؟" قال: "ثم الْموتُ." قال: "فالآنَ من قريب. ربِّ إمِتني من الأرضِ الْمُقدّسةِ رميةً بحَجَر."

فشمّهُ شمّةً فقبضَ روحَه. فجاء بعد ذلكَ إلى الناسِ خفِيّاً.»

‹When the angel told Moosaa this, Moosaa asked Allaah (ﷻ), "What after that long life, my Lord?" Allaah revealed to Moosaa, "After that, you will die." Moosaa said, "Then, let it be now. And my Lord, let me die a stone's throw away from the Holy Land [1]." So with one sniff, the Angel of Death took Moosaa's soul. After this incident, the Angel of Death always came to people in an invisible form.›

The Prophet Muhammad (ﷺ) then added:

«ولو أنّي عِندهُ لأريتُكم قبرَه إِلَى جانِبِ الطريقِ تحت الكَثيبِ الأحْمَرِ.»

‹If I was near that place, I would have shown you his grave by the road at the foot of the red mountain.› [2]

1 This means Jerusalem.

2 This *hadeeth* is recorded by al-Bukhaaree, Muslim, Ahmad, and others from Aboo Hurayrah (see *as-Saheehah* no. 3279).

THE HELPERS OF THE ANGEL OF DEATH

There are other angels who accompany the Angel of Death when he takes the souls from the bodies. They come with him when a person is close to death. Allaah (ﷻ) says about them:

﴿حَتَّىٰٓ إِذَا جَآءَ أَحَدَكُمُ ٱلْمَوْتُ تَوَفَّتْهُ رُسُلُنَا وَهُمْ لَا يُفَرِّطُونَ﴾ الأنعام ٦١

«When death comes to one of you, Our messengers (the angels) take his soul, and they never neglect their duty.» [1]

There are many *hadeeth*s about the Angel of Death and his helpers. For example, the Prophet (ﷺ) said:

«تلقّتِ الْمَلائِكَةُ رُوحَ رَجُلٍ مِمّن كانَ قَبْلَكُم، فقالوا: "عمِلتَ مَن الْخَيرِ شيئاً؟" قال: "لا، غيرَ أنّي كُنتُ أداينُ الناسِ، فأُنظِرُ الْموسِرَ، وأتجاوزُ عن الْمُعْسِرِ. لعلّ اللهَ يتجاوزُ عنّي." فقال اللهُ تعالَى: "أنا أحقُّ بذلِك مِنك. تجاوزوا عن عبدي."»

‹The angels took the soul of a man from the previous nations. They asked him, "Have you done any good deeds?" He said, "No, except that I used to lend money to people, and I was easy in demanding repayment from the

1 *Soorat al-An'aam* 6:61.

wealthy, and I pardoned the poor, hoping that Allaah (ﷻ) would pardon me." Allaah then said, "I have more right to pardon than you." And He commanded the angels, "Pardon my servant."› [1]

There are two types of these angels of death: the angels of mercy and the angels of punishment. They are both mentioned by the Prophet (ﷺ) in the following story:

«كان فيمن كان قبلكم رجُلٌ قتل تسعةً وتسعينَ نفساً، فسأَلَ عن أعلَم أهلِ الأرض، فدُلَّ على راهِب، فأتاهُ فقال إنَّهُ قتل تسعةً وتِسعين نفساً، فهل له مِن توبة؟ فقال: "لا." فقتلَه فكمَّل بهِ مِئَةً. ثم سأل عن أعلمِ أهلِ الأرض، فدُلَ على رجُل عالِم، فقال إنّه قتل مئةَ نفسٍ، فهل له من توبة؟ فقال: "نعم، من يَحولُ بينك وبين التوبةِ؟ أنطلِق إلى أرضِ كذا وكذا، فإنّ بها أُناساً يعبُدونَ اللهَ، فاعبدِ اللهَ معهُم، ولا ترجِعْ إلى أرضِك، فإنّها أرضُ سوءٍ." فانطلقَ، حتى إذا نَصفَ الطريقَ أتاهُ الْموتُ، فاختصَمَت فيهِ ملائكةُ الرحمةِ وملائكةُ

1 Recorded by al-Bukhaaree and Muslim from Hu<u>th</u>ayfah and Aboo Hurayrah (رضي الله عنهما).

العذاب، فقالت ملائكةُ الرحْمةِ: "جاء تائباً مُقبِلاً بقلبه إلى اللهِ تعالَى." وقالَت ملائكةُ العذاب: "إنّه لم يعملْ خيراً قط." فأتاهم مَلَكٌ في صورةِ آدمِيّ فجعَلوه بينَهُم، فقال: "قيسوا ما بينَ الأرضين، فإلَى أيَّتهُما كان أدنى فهُوَ له." فقاسوا فوجدوه أدنى إلَى الأرض التي أرادَ، فقبَضتهُ ملائكةُ الرحْمَةِ.»

‹A man from the people who lived before you killed ninety-nine persons. He wanted to repent, so he asked who was the most learned person on earth. He was directed to a monk. He went to him and told him that he had killed ninety-nine persons, and asked if he may repent. The monk said, "No!" The man killed him, making this his hundredth murder.

Still wishing to repent, the man again asked who was the most learned person on earth. He was directed to a *'aalim* (scholar). He went to him and told him that he had killed one hundred

persons, and asked if he may repent. The *'aalim* answered, "Certainly! Who can prevent you from repenting? Go to such-and-such town. You will find people who worship Allaah, so worship Him with them, and do not return to your land because it is an evil land."

Following the *'aalim*'s advice, the man started in the direction of the good town. When he was near the middle of the way, he suddenly died.

The angels of mercy and the angels of punishment disputed over him. The angels of mercy said, "He came repenting, his heart turning to Allaah (سبحانه وتعالى)." The angels of punishment said, "But he never did a good deed."

Allaah then sent an angel in the form of a man to resolve the dispute. He said, "Measure his distance to each of the two lands, and consider that he belonged to the land nearer to him."

They did this and found him just a little nearer to the good land. So, the angels of mercy took his soul.› [1]

1 This *hadeeth* is recorded by al-Bukhaaree, Muslim, and others from Aboo Sa'eed al-Khudree (رضي الله عنه).

THE ANGELS OF MERCY

The angels of mercy come to the believers at the time of death in a kind manner. They remove their souls kindly and tell them of their great rewards in *Jannah*. Allaah (ﷻ) says:

﴿إِنَّ ٱلَّذِينَ قَالُواْ رَبُّنَا ٱللَّهُ ثُمَّ ٱسْتَقَٰمُواْ تَتَنَزَّلُ عَلَيْهِمُ ٱلْمَلَٰٓئِكَةُ أَلَّا تَخَافُواْ وَلَا تَحْزَنُواْ وَأَبْشِرُواْ بِٱلْجَنَّةِ ٱلَّتِي كُنتُمْ تُوعَدُونَ ۝ نَحْنُ أَوْلِيَآؤُكُمْ فِي ٱلْحَيَوٰةِ ٱلدُّنْيَا وَفِي ٱلْأَخِرَةِ...﴾ فصلت ٣٠-٣١

«Surely, those who say, "Our Lord is Allaah Alone," and do good, the angels descend to them (at the time of death) saying, "Do not be afraid or sad. We bring you the good news of the *Jannah* that you have been promised. We have been your friends in the life of this world, and will be so in the hereafter ...» [1]

THE ANGELS OF PUNISHMENT

The angels of punishment come to the disbelievers at the time of death in a cruel and horrible manner. They tear out their souls and beat them hard. Allaah (ﷻ) says:

﴿فَكَيْفَ إِذَا تَوَفَّتْهُمُ ٱلْمَلَٰٓئِكَةُ يَضْرِبُونَ وُجُوهَهُمْ وَأَدْبَٰرَهُمْ ۝﴾ محمد ٢٧

1 *Soorat Fussilat* 41:30-32.

«Then how will it be when the angels will take their souls at death, beating their faces and backs?» [1]

Maalik and the Guards of Hell

The guards of Hell keep it hot and burning for the evil people. Their leader is called Maalik. Allaah (ﷻ) says:

﴿فَلْيَدْعُ نَادِيَهُۥ ۝ سَنَدْعُ ٱلزَّبَانِيَةَ ۝﴾ العلق ١٧-١٨

«Then let him (Aboo Jahl) call upon his helpers: We will call the guards of Hell (to deal with him).» [2]

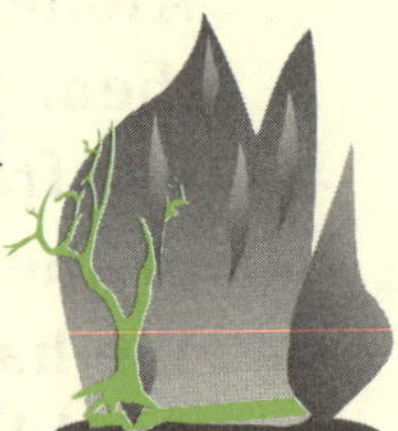

Maalik has no mercy or kindness toward the *kuffaar*. Allaah (ﷻ) says:

﴿وَنَادَوْاْ يَـٰمَـٰلِكُ لِيَقْضِ عَلَيْنَا رَبُّكَ قَالَ إِنَّكُم مَّـٰكِثُونَ ۝
لَقَدْ جِئْنَـٰكُم بِٱلْحَقِّ وَلَـٰكِنَّ أَكْثَرَكُمْ لِلْحَقِّ كَـٰرِهُونَ ۝﴾

الزخرف ٧٧-٧٨

«And they (the people of the Fire) will cry, "O Maalik! Let your Lord make an end of us." He will say, "You will stay! Indeed, We have brought the truth to you, but most of

1 *Soorat Muhammad* 47:27.
2 *Soorat al-'Alaq* 96:17-18.

you (people) have a hatred for the truth." » [1]

Munkar and Nakeer

Munkar and Nakeer are two angels whose job is to question the people in their grave. They ask them about their Lord, their religion, and about the Prophet Muhammad (ﷺ). The believers give right answers to these questions, which result in a restful stay in the grave. The disbelievers give wrong answers, which result in their punishment in the grave. [2] The Prophet (ﷺ) said:

«إذا قُبِرَ الْمَيِّتُ أتاهُ مَلَكانِ أسودانِ أزرقان، يُقال لأحدِهِما الْمُنكَرُ، والآخرُ النّكيرُ.»

‹When a dead person is buried, two black-blue angels come to him. One of them is called Munkar, and the other Nakeer.› [3]

Haaroot and Maaroot

Haaroot and Maaroot are two angels that Allaah (ﷻ) mentions in the Qur'aan [4]. He sent them to an old city

---

1 *Soorat az-Zukhruf* 63:77-78.

2 This is discussed in detail in the Author's book, "Life in *al-Barzakh*".

3 Recorded by at-Tirmithee from Aboo Hurayrah. Verified to be *hasan* by al-Albaanee (*Saheeh ul-Jaami'* no. 724 and *as-Saheehah* no. 1391).

4 *Soorat al-Baqarah* 2:102.

called Babylon where the devils taught its people black magic. The two angels showed the people a more powerful magic, but warned them, "If you insist on learning this from us, you should know that we have only been sent to try you with this knowledge. Magic often leads to disbelief in Allaah and to evil."

The devils and the evil people learned from these two angels magic that enabled them to break-up families and caused great harm on earth. By that, they deserved Allaah's anger and punishment.

Conclusion

Correct belief in the angels helps us know these sublime and righteous beings. It also teaches us what we should do to deserve their love, help, and support.

With this belief, we also understand that those who obey Allaah (ﷻ) are many more than those who do not. They include the angels and multitudes of other created things. The disobedient humans are indeed very few compared to them.

And indeed, Allaah (ﷻ) only loves the obedient, and will only admit them into His *Jannah*. May He make us of them, *aameen*.

Questions and Exercises

1. In the following table, check all true statements (41 points):

	Statement	✓
a	The first time that the Prophet (ﷺ) saw Jibreel was in his house in Makkah.	
b	Jibreel went with the Prophet (ﷺ) to the seventh heaven.	
c	*Al-Israa'* was the trip from Makkah to al-Madeenah.	
d	*Al-Mi'raaj* was the trip from Makkah to Jerusalem.	
e	The Prophet (ﷺ) knew how to perform *wudoo'* and pray since he was a child.	
f	The Prophet (ﷺ) was the most generous person.	
g	Jibreel learned Qur'aan from the Prophet (ﷺ).	
h	Jibreel often gave advice to the Prophet (ﷺ).	
i	Moosaa (عليه السلام) was afraid to die.	
j	Allaah is kind to those who are kind to the poor.	
k	Allaah does not accept the repentance of a killer.	
l	The Angel of Death is called 'Izraa'eel.	
m	The angels of mercy take the souls of the believers.	

	Statement	✓
n	The people in the Fire will be allowed to die.	
o	Munkar and Nakeer take the disbelievers's souls.	
p	The disbelievers' souls are removed harshly at death.	
q	The Prophet (ﷺ) saw Jibreel in his original form every Friday.	
r	There is a tree by Allaah's Throne.	
s	There are pearls on Jibreel's garments.	
t	Jibreel liked to speak to Duhyah al-Kalbee.	
u	The soil of *Jannah* is made of musk.	
v	An angel performed surgery for the Prophet (ﷺ).	
w	Jibreel does not need permission to enter into the heavens.	
x	Faatimah (رضي الله عنها) died shortly before the Prophet (ﷺ).	
y	A Muslim should be kind to his neighbors.	
z	The Prophet (ﷺ) learned things from both Jibreel and Meekaa'eel.	
A	Jibreel shook hands with Khadeejah and 'Aa'ishah.	
B	When the Prophet (ﷺ) was sick, Jibreel said a *du'aa* for him.	
C	Meekaa'eel is the most humorous angel.	

	Statement	✓
D	Israafeel is mentioned in the Qur'aan.	
E	Israafeel is probably the Horn Blower.	
F	The Horn Blower will get ready to blow it after the return of 'Eesaa.	
G	The Horn Blower never blinks.	
H	The Angel of Death used to come in human form.	
I	Moosaa had the choice to live thousands of years.	
J	Moosaa died very close to Jerusalem.	
K	The angels never dispute among each other.	
L	Haaroot and Maaroot came to Babylon.	
M	Among Allaah's creation, the obedient are less than the disobedient.	
N	The Prophet's (ﷺ) heart was filled with wisdom.	
O	It is important to live among righteous people.	

2. Mention 6 qualities of Jibreel as in *Soorat at-Takweer* (12 points):

1	4
2	5
3	6

3. Mention 2 of Jibreel's names in the Qur'aan (4 points):

1	2

4. Match between the angels and their jobs in the following two lists. Note that the option "No authentic mention" applies to angels who were not named in the Qu'aan or authentic Sunnah, yet many people give them certain names. (8 points)

Meekaa'eel	
Israafeel	No authentic mention
Radhwaan	
Maalik	Try people in the grave
Haaroot & Maaroot	In charge of Hell
Munkar & Nakeer	Blow the Horn
Raqeeb & 'Ateed	Brings rain and food
Izraa'eel	Tried the people with magic

ARABIC VOCABULARY

Term	Meaning
Aayah	Approximately one sentence of the Qur'aan. Plural: *aayaat*.
'Aalim	Scholar. Plural: *'Ulamaa'*.
'Abd	Servant of (Allaah).
Al-Ka'bah	The House of worship in Makkah. All of the Muslims face it in their prayers.
Al-Madeenah	The town in Arabia where the Prophet (ﷺ) built his mosque and lived the last ten years of his life.
Deen	Religion.
Eemaan	Faith or belief.
Hadeeth	A saying or an action of the Prophet (ﷺ).
Hajj	Pilgrimage.
Ihsaan	Worshiping and fearing Allaah as if you can see Him.
Jahannam	The hell fire.

Term	Meaning
Jannah	The gardens of Paradise.
Jinn	Invisible creatures that Allaah created from smoke.
Kaafir	One who does not believe in Islaam. Plural: *kuffaar*.
Khutbah	Speech.
Makkah	The hometown of the Prophet (ﷺ).
Masjid	Mosque. Place where the Muslims pray.
Mu'min	Believer or one who has *eemaan*.
Qadar	Destiny or decree.
Ramadhaan	The month of fasting.
Sahaabee	Companion of the Prophet (ﷺ). Plural: *Sahaabah*.
Salaah	The prayer.
Salaf	Early good Muslims.
Shahaadah	Testimony.
Sujood	Putting the forehead down on the ground in prayer to Allaah.
Sunnah	The Prophet's teachings.

Term	Meaning
Soorah	Chapter of the Qur'aan.
Tafseer	Explanation of the *Qur'aan.*
Thikr	Mentioning Allaah by heart and tongue. Plural: *athkaar*.
Zakaah	Obligatory charity in Islaam.

PUBLISHED TITLES BY THE AUTHOR

Fiqh Handbooks

1. Festivals & Celebrations in Islām, 2nd Ed., 272 pp, 2005.
2. The Night Prayers, *Qiyām* & *Tarāwīh*, 2nd Ed., 195 pp, 1999.

The Inevitable Journey

1. Sickness, Regulations and Exhortations, 2nd Ed., 327 pp, HB, 2003.
2. Inheritance, Regulations and Exhortations, 2nd Ed., 175 pp, HB, 2005.

2a. Islāmic Will & Testament Booklet, 16 pp, 2000.

3. Funerals, Regulations and Exhortations, 2nd Ed., 326 pp, HB, 2003.
4. Life in *al-Barzakh*, from Death until Resurrection, 2nd Ed., 269 pp, 2006.
5. The Dreamer's Handbook, Sleep Etiquettes & Dream Interpretation, 360 pp, HB, 2006.

The Muslim Family

1. Quest for Love & Mercy (Regulations for Marriage & Wedding in Islām), Rev. Ed., 204 pp, 2005.
2. Closer than a Garment (Marital Intimacy According to the Pure Sunnah), Rev. Ed., 192 pp, 2005.
3. The Fragile Vessels (Rights & Obligations Between the Spouses in Islām), Rev. Ed., 190 pp, 2005.
4. Our Precious Sprouts (Islāmic Regulations for Newborns), 234 pp, 2002.

Īmān Made Easy

1. Knowing Allāh, 2nd Ed., 127 pp, 2002.
2. Knowing the Angels, 2nd Ed., 131 pp, 2003.
3. Knowing Allāh's Books & the Qur'ān, 2nd Ed., 124 pp, 2003.
4. Knowing Allāh's Prophets & Messengers, 127 pp, 2002.
5. Knowing the Last Day, 216 pp, 2004.
6. Believing in Allāh's Decree, *Qadar*, 247 pp, 2004.

Enter Into Islām Completely

1. The Beard & Other Traits of *Fiṭrah*, 2nd Ed., 111 pp, 2005.
2. Smoking, a Social Poison, 51 pp, 1999.
3. Islāmic Perspective of Contraception & Abortion, 64 pp, 2000.
4. Regulations of Worship During Menses, 86 pp, 2001.

Stories from the Sunnah

1. Ibrāhīm, A Nation in One Man, 184 pp, 2003.

Other Titles

1. *Ar-Risālat ut-Tabūkiyyah* (the Magnificent Journey), 2nd Ed., 136 pp, 2001.
2. Commanding Good & Forbidding Evil According to Ibn Taymiyyah, 54 pp, 1997.
3. Allāh's Right upon His Servants: *Tawḥīd* vs. *Shirk*, 51 pp, 1995 (out of print).
4. The Qur'ān and the Sunnah, 38 pp, 1982 (out of print).